THE ITALIAN'S BRIDE
Commanded—to be his wife!

Used to the finest food, clothes and women, these immensely powerful, incredibly good-looking and undeniably charismatic men have only one last need: a wife!

They've chosen their brides-to-be and they'll have them—willing or not!

Enjoy all of our fantastic stories this month:

The Italian Billionaire's Secret Love-Child
Cathy Williams

Sicilian Millionaire, Bought Bride
Catherine Spencer

Bedded and Wedded for Revenge
Melanie Milburne

The Italian's Unwilling Wife
Kathryn Ross

Happy holidays from
Harlequin Presents EXTRA!

KATHRYN ROSS was born in Zambia to an English father and an Irish mother. She was educated in Ireland and England, where she later worked as a professional beauty therapist before becoming a full-time writer.

Most of her childhood was spent in a small village in southern Ireland; she said it was a wonderful place to grow up, surrounded by the spectacular beauty of the Wicklow Mountains and the rugged coastline of the Irish Sea. She feels that living in Ireland first sparked off her desire to write; it was so rich in both scenery and warm characters that it invited her to put pen to paper.

Kathryn doesn't remember a time when she wasn't scribbling. As a child she wrote adventure stories and a one-act play that won a competition. She became editor of her school magazine, which she said gave her great training for working into the night and meeting deadlines. Happily, ten years later, Harlequin accepted her first book, *Designed With Love,* for publication.

Kathryn loves to travel and seek out exotic locations for her books. She feels it helps her writing to be able to set her scenes against backgrounds that she has visited. Traveling and meeting people also give her great inspiration. That's how all her novels start: she gets a spark of excitement from some incident or conversation and that sets her imagination working. Her characters are always a pastiche of people she has either met or read about, or would like to meet. She likes being a novelist because she can make things happen—well, most of the time, anyhow. Sometimes her characters take over and do things that surprise even her!

At present Kathryn is working on her next book, and can be found walking her dogs in the Lake District in England as she thinks about her plots.

THE ITALIAN'S UNWILLING WIFE

KATHRYN ROSS

~ THE ITALIAN'S BRIDE ~

HARLEQUIN®

TORONTO • NEW YORK • LONDON
AMSTERDAM • PARIS • SYDNEY • HAMBURG
STOCKHOLM • ATHENS • TOKYO • MILAN • MADRID
PRAGUE • WARSAW • BUDAPEST • AUCKLAND

ISBN-13: 978-0-373-82382-6
ISBN-10:   0-373-82382-7

THE ITALIAN'S UNWILLING WIFE

First North American Publication 2008.

www.eHarlequin.com

Printed in U.S.A.

THE ITALIAN'S
UNWILLING WIFE

PROLOGUE

REVENGE was an ugly word. Damon Cyrenci preferred to think of his actions in more clinical terms. He had seen a business opportunity and had taken it.

The fact that he'd had his eye on the Newland Company for a while, and that this takeover gave him a greater sense of personal satisfaction than any other, was irrelevant. What was important was that John Newland's days of trampling his opponents into dust were almost at an end.

As his chauffeured limousine travelled along the Strip, Damon watched the sun setting in a pink glow over the Las Vegas skyline. This was the city where his father had lost everything. It was also the city where Damon had made the mistake of allowing a woman to get under his skin. It seemed fitting that it should be the place where he would put everything right, get back what he wanted.

They passed the MGM Grand, Caesar's Palace, New York New York and, as the pink of the sky turned to the darkness of night, the desert lit up with fiercely glittering light.

The limousine pulled up outside the impressive façade of the Newland building, and Damon allowed himself to savour the moment. His target was almost achieved. In a few moments he would meet John Newland face to face, and have him exactly where he wanted him.

For a second his thoughts drifted back to the last time they had met. How different that meeting had been.

Two and a half years ago it was John who had held the balance of power. He had faced Damon across a boardroom table and had calmly refused his request for a stay of execution on his father's business.

One week—that was all Damon had needed in order to release valuable assets that were in his name and save everything. But Newland had been coldly adamant. 'I am not a charity, Cyrenci; I'm in the business of making money. Your father must honour his commitments immediately and hand over the title deeds to all of his properties. However...' He'd paused for a moment's reflection. 'Your family home in Sicily is listed as one of the company's assets. I might allow you to keep that—on one condition.'

'And what's that?' Damon had asked coolly.

'You walk away from my daughter and never see her again.'

Damon could remember his incredulity and the hot fury in his stomach as he had looked across at the man. Somehow he had remained calm and impassive. 'I am not going to do that.'

And that was when John Newland had laughed at him. 'Abbie really fooled you, didn't she? Let me enlighten you, Cyrenci. My daughter has been brought up with a certain standard of living. She enjoys a luxurious lifestyle—a lifestyle you can't match now the family business has gone. I assure you, she won't be interested in you now.'

'That's a risk I'll take,' Damon had told him smoothly.

'Your choice.' John Newland had shrugged. 'But you lose all ways round. Abbie only dated you in the first place as a favour to me. I needed you out of my hair, and she was the perfect distraction. You think your weekend away together in Palm Springs was a wild impulse?'

John had asked the question scornfully and had shaken his head. 'It was planned—all set up by me. Abbie knew I needed some time to finish my business with your father, and she was happy to help me—but then, just as long as the money is flowing, Abbie will be there. Believe me, she won't hang around you now the game is over and your money is gone.'

The chauffeur opened up the passenger door for Damon, letting in the intense heat of the desert night, a heat almost as intense as the anger he had felt back then. It hadn't been hard to discover that for once John Newland was telling the truth. Abbie had known what her father had been up to, and had in fact assisted him.

Just like her father, she was nothing but a cold-blooded, money-grabbing trickster.

Snapping out of his reverie, Damon stepped out of the limousine.

It had been a lesson hard learnt. But Damon had picked himself up and with strong determination he had seen to it that their fortunes had been reversed.

Briskly he walked up the red-carpeted steps into the cool of the air-conditioned foyer. The entrance to the Newland hotel and casino was palatial; gold-leafed ceilings and stained-glass windows gave it the air of a cathedral, and only the rolling sound of nearby slot machines revealed the truth.

With just a cursory nod to the hotel staff, he headed for the lifts. He knew his way to the boardroom and he strode with confidence towards the door he wanted. This was the moment he had been waiting for.

John Newland was sitting alone at the far end of the long polished table. The lighting in the room was dimmed, his face in shadow. Behind him the picture windows gave a panoramic view of Vegas, glittering like a mirror-ball in the night. But Damon wasn't interested in the view.

'I believe you are expecting me.' He closed the door quietly behind him.

There was silence.

Damon advanced until he could see his nemesis clearly: grey-haired, thickset with glittering hooded eyes. The last time they had met, the man's features had been alight with triumphant disdain. Today, however, his expression was carefully schooled, but Damon could see the signs of strain in the pallor of his skin and the tight way he held his mouth.

It was hard to believe that this was Abigail's father. For a second a picture of her drifted into Damon's mind.

He remembered the day he had met her. She had been swimming here in the hotel pool, and he had watched as she'd pulled herself out. Water had dripped in silver beads over her toned skin. He remembered the sensational curves of her body in the scanty bikini, the perfection of her features, the wide blue eyes, the softness of her lips.

How he had wanted her.

The sudden memory of how badly he had wanted her made heat rise inside him.

'You're early, Cyrenci. The board isn't due to meet for another half an hour.'

John Newland's terse words focussed Damon's thoughts back to where they should be. He would have time to concentrate on Abbie later.

'We both know that the board meeting is just a formality, Newland.' Damon put his briefcase down on the table and opened it. 'You are on your way out.'

John Newland blanched. 'Look—Damon—we've had our differences in the past. But I hope we can put all that behind us and perhaps come to some mutually acceptable deal.' The brusque tone was gone now, replaced by pure desperation. 'I've spoken to a few members of the board—'

'It's over,' Damon said coolly. 'I think you would be advised to just accept that.'

'But you could help me if you wanted to.'

Was the man serious? Damon looked at him with incredulity. 'Why would I do that? To quote something you said to me years ago, John: I'm a businessman, not a charity.'

'I have a few bargaining chips left.' The man shrugged.

'Such as?' Damon was barely listening. He was taking papers out of his case and his eyes were running down a list of the company's assets—assets that now belonged to him. He knew John Newland held no aces, because they were all right here in his hand.

'Well—I recall you once wanted my daughter…'

The words trailed away as Damon fixed him with a cool, penetrating stare. He could hardly believe what he was hearing.

'In fact, you wanted her so badly you were willing to give up your family home for her,' John reminded him tentatively.

'We all make mistakes.' Damon's voice was icy.

'She had her twenty-first birthday last week, and I assure you she is even more beautiful now than she was,' John Newland continued swiftly. 'And her mother was Lady Annabel Redford, you know. Abbie has some influential connections in England that could open doors to a businessman like you.'

'I'm not interested.'

'I think you should be. And if I were to have a word with her…'

'Still at Daddy's bidding, is she?' Damon remarked scathingly.

'I have influence.'

'You have nothing.' Damon put his list of the company assets down on the table in front of the man.

'That's her, isn't it—the property that's marked a few lines underneath my old family home in Sicily?' Damon pointed to a line almost at the bottom of the page. 'Redford Stables, St Lucia.'

John Newland made no reply, just stared down at the list.

'Do you think Abbie will be happy to assist you, John, when she finds out her luxurious lifestyle and her home are lost as part of the company's assets?'

Still the man made no reply, but he started to drum his fingers with agitation against the table.

'No, I didn't think so. As we both know, Abbie's loyalty is to the highest bidder. So I don't believe you or indeed your daughter are in any position to negotiate,' Damon continued smoothly. 'But rest assured I will be looking over my new property with close attention to detail. In fact, I'm heading out to St Lucia tomorrow. Have you any message you would like me to pass on to your daughter?'

There was a moment's considered silence before John looked up. 'No, but I have one for your son—tell him his granddad says hello.'

John Newland watched the shock hit Damon Cyrenci and felt a gleam of satisfaction.

CHAPTER ONE

IT WAS hurricane season in St Lucia and the warnings had gone out. 'Michael' was a category three, but was gathering pace at sea and heading for shore. The weathermen were predicating a direct hit sometime within the next twenty-four hours.

But for now the sun was setting in a perfect blaze of glory over the lush rainforests, and not a breath of air rustled the tall palms that encircled the stables.

Abbie, however, was not taken in by the deceptive calm. She had experienced the full force of a hurricane the previous year; it had taken the roof off her house and almost decimated the stables. It had taken a long time to put everything right, and financially she was still reeling from the disaster. She couldn't afford another direct hit.

So she had spent the afternoon trying to prepare. She had nailed down everything she could, and long after most of her hired help had gone home for the day she was still moving heavy equipment into the storerooms.

'Abbie, your father has been on the phone for you again,' Jess called across to her as she came out of the house. 'He's left another message on the answer machine.'

'OK, thanks.' Abbie brushed her blonde hair distractedly back from her face. She had nothing to say to her father, and she wasn't interested in his messages, but she couldn't help but wonder why he had started ringing her again.

Putting the last of her work tools away, she headed up to the veranda. Mario was in Jess's arms, and as he saw his mother walk towards them his eyes lit with excitement and he held out his arms to her.

With a smile, Abbie reached to take her baby. He snuggled in against her and she kissed him, breathing in the clean scent of his skin. Mario was twenty-one months now, and adorable. He was the one thing in Abbie's life that made everything worthwhile.

'Do you want to get off now, Jess? You've got a date tonight, haven't you?' she asked as she cuddled the child.

'Yes. If you are sure you can manage, that would be a great help.'

'Absolutely. You go and have a good time.'

For a moment Abbie stood and watched as the young woman strolled towards her four-wheel drive. At eighteen, Jess was the youngest member of her staff, and also the hardest working. Not only was she a qualified child-minder and a superb horse-woman but she helped out a lot around the stables. Sometimes Abbie wondered how she would manage without her.

She waved to Jess as she reversed and pulled away down the long driveway.

Darkness was closing in now. The stables were on a lonely track leading down to a deserted cove. Her nearest neighbours were miles away, and very few cars passed this way. Usually Abbie didn't mind being on her own; she enjoyed the solitude. But for once as Jess's car disappeared she was acutely conscious of her isolation.

It was probably the approaching storm that was making her feel so on edge, she told herself as she went back into the house. Plus all these phone calls from her father.

As she stepped inside, her eyes were immediately drawn towards the phone, where a flashing light proclaimed there were now ten messages.

Whatever her father wanted, she wasn't interested. She would put Mario to bed and delete the calls later, she told herself as she headed for the stairs.

The child went down into his cot easily. Abbie set the musical mobile playing above his head and watched over him until he fell asleep. Then, leaving the night light on, she crept from the nursery to her bedroom across the corridor to shower and change.

Abbie had just put on her silk dressing-gown and was about to go back downstairs to make herself a drink when the phone in her room rang again, and the answer machine clicked on.

'Abbie, where the hell are you?' Her father's irate tones seemed to fill the house. *'Have you received any of my messages? This is important.'*

It was strange how just hearing his voice made her nervous. She supposed it was all those years of conditioning—of being afraid to ignore his commands.

Wrapping her dressing gown more closely around her body, she reminded herself fiercely that her father no longer had a hold over her—he couldn't hurt her any more.

'Do you hear me, Abigail?'

He probably wanted to summon her back to Vegas to host one of his parties. She shuddered at the thought. She'd escaped from that life over two years ago—she would have thought he'd got the message by now. His bullying blackmail tactics no longer worked. She wasn't going back.

She was on her way across her bedroom to switch off the machine when she heard him mention a name—a name that made her freeze and the world start to zone out as darkness threatened to engulf her. *Damon Cyrenci.*

For so long she had tried to block that name out of her mind, pretend he had never existed. And the only way she had been able to do that was by filling her every waking hour and making herself so bone-tired that personal thoughts were a luxury. But, even so, sometimes in the silence of the night he would come to her as she slept and she would see his darkly handsome face again. Would imagine his hands touching her, his lips crushing against hers, and she would wake with tears on her cheeks.

'I've lost everything, Abigail—everything—to Damon Cyrenci, and that includes the stables because they are part of the company's assets.'

Through the turmoil of her thoughts, Abbie tried to concentrate on what her father was saying. The stables were hers, weren't they?

'And he's on his way out there now to look over his property.'

The words hit her like a hurricane at force five. Damon was on his way here! Her heart raced—her body felt weak. Damon—the love of her life, the father of her child, the one man she had given herself to completely. The memories that went along with all those facts twisted inside her like a serpent intent on squeezing her very soul. And along with the memories there was a fierce longing—a longing that had never really gone away, a longing that she had just learnt to live with.

She sat down on the bed behind her; it was either sit down or fall down. *Damon was coming here.* It was all she could focus on.

What would he look like now, what would he say to her? Would he still be angry with her? What would he say when he discovered he had a child?

Had he forgiven her? The wrench of yearning that idea brought with it was immense.

As the phone connection died, she buried her head in her hands.

She remembered the day she had first met Damon. She remembered that the blistering heat of the midday sun had come nowhere near matching the heat he had stirred within her. She remembered shading her eyes to look up at him as she'd climbed out of the pool. He was tall—well over six-foot-four and he had been wearing a lightweight suit that had sat perfectly on his athletic build.

'You must be Abbie Newland?' he had said quietly, and the attractive accent had added fuel to a fire that had quietly and instantly started to blaze inside her.

He was ten years older than Abbie, Sicilian, with thick dark hair and searing, intense dark eyes, and to say he was good-looking would be an understatement of vast proportions. He was quite simply gorgeous.

'I'm Damon Cyrenci. Your father said I would find you here.'

The disappointment inside Abbie was almost as intense as her attraction for him. Because this was the man her father had ordered her to date. The command had infuriated her, but she wasn't at liberty to refuse; her plan had been to snub him, then just walk away. Then she could honestly tell her father that he hadn't invited her out. But, as soon as her eyes met with the handsome Sicilian, her body didn't want to comply with that idea at all.

'Do you want to join me for a drink?' He nodded over towards a bar that was cocooned in the tropical shade of the gardens.

'Maybe just for ten minutes,' she found herself saying. 'I haven't got much time.'

'Why, what else have you got to do?' The question had been asked with a glint of humour, and it had been apparent right from the outset that he had judged her as little more than a social butterfly.

She didn't really blame him. To the outside world, that was probably exactly how her life appeared, but the remark still smarted. She wanted to tell him that appearances could be deceptive, that she was in fact trapped within her gilded cage, forced to dance attendance on a father whose every whim was her command. But of course she didn't—he wouldn't have been interested and anyway, if word got back to her father that she had said anything, the consequences would have been dire.

So somehow she just forced herself to shrug. 'Let's see. I'm the rich, spoilt daughter of a millionaire—what else could I be doing this afternoon?' She slanted him a sardonic look. 'Apart from lying in the sun, shopping and visiting the beauty salon, you mean?'

He smiled, unapologetic. 'Must be a tough life.'

'It is. But someone has to do it.' Although she tried to sound flippant, something of her annoyance or distress must have shown in her eyes, because suddenly his tone softened.

'Shall we start again?' he asked, and held out his hand. 'I'm Damon Cyrenci, and I'm in town to negotiate the sale of a chain of restaurants owned by my father.'

She looked at the hand he held out, and she hesitated a moment before taking it. What exactly was her father up to? she had wondered. What harm would following his orders do?

Then her eyes met with Damon Cyrenci's and she told herself that, no matter what her father was up to, this man was more than capable of looking out for himself.

'Abigail Newland.' The net was cast as she placed her hand in his. She liked the touch of his skin against hers, liked the feeling in the pit of her stomach when he smiled.

She remembered having dinner with him that night. She remembered him kissing her, a searing, intensely passionate kiss that had made her long for so much more.

She had dated him for five short weeks, but with each meeting her feelings for him had intensified. Her hands curled into tight fists just thinking about the way he'd made her feel. But because of the situation she had always forced herself to pull back.

Damon hadn't been used to a woman pulling away from him, and somehow it had made him all the more determined to pursue her.

Yes, the net had been cast—but she had been the one caught in its fine weave, because somewhere along the way in those few short weeks she had fallen in love with Damon Cyrenci.

The phone rang again, interrupting Abbie's thoughts, and she listened as once more the answer machine cut in.

'Abbie, please pick up the phone.'

Abbie just sat numbly, listening. She hadn't spoken to her father since her mother's death just over two years ago. And, no matter what was at stake, she still couldn't speak to him now.

'This is about revenge, Abigail—and you are next on Cyrenci's list. He knows what you did—knows you were perfectly complicit in his father's destruction.' Her father's voice was abrasive. *'But luckily I'm still thinking for both of us. I told him about Mario. He was shocked and angry, I could see it in his face. But the child gives us a bargaining chip—it means he doesn't hold all of the aces.'*

Abbie felt sick inside. She hated her father—hated the sordid, horrible way he even thought.

The line went dead again. Abbie didn't know how long she just sat there after that. Her father stopped phoning, but the silence of the house seemed to swirl around her with his words.

Then she heard the distant sound of a car engine.

He's on his way out there now to look over his property...

Certainly, whoever was in that car was heading for this house—there was nowhere else out here.

CHAPTER TWO

THE shrill ring of the doorbell cut through her. And for a few moments she was immobilised.

Was Damon really outside her door? There had been moments when she had dreamed of this, dreamed that he'd come to her when he found out about his child, and that he would forgive her.

But they were just dreams. She was sensible enough to realise that the reality was encapsulated in her father's phone messages.

Damon wasn't going to forgive her—she'd known that at their last meeting, when he had angrily confronted her about what she had done, and she had tried desperately to explain her actions. He hadn't wanted to listen; all he'd been able to think about was the fact that she had assisted in his father's downfall. Even when she had falteringly tried to tell him that she was as much a victim as his father he had cut across her contemptuously.

'You must consider me really naïve if you think I'm going to fall for any more of your lies. I know what you are. I have evidence to support exactly what a lying, conniving, deceitful—'

'Damon, please!' She had broken across him tremulously.

'Please believe me, I never wanted any of this to happen. The time I spent with you was special to me, and I—'

'Give the acting a rest, Abbie.' The scorn in his voice had cut through her like a sword. 'At least the one good thing about this whole sorry mess is the fact that, as far as I was concerned, our time together was all about sex—I felt nothing for you, other than the pleasure of taking your body. Nothing at all.'

There had been a harsh coldness in his words and in his eyes that she had never seen before. It was as if a mask had been ripped away at that moment and she had seen the true Damon for the first time. It had shocked her to the core, and it had hurt. God help her, it still hurt!

But it also made her very sure that if it was Damon outside he wasn't here for any sentimental reasons, and he certainly wouldn't be interested in the fact that she'd had his child.

The shrill ring of the doorbell sliced through the night again, and Abbie tried to focus on what she should do. There were a few heartbeats of silence whilst whoever it was gave her a moment to come to the door. When she didn't, he put his finger on the bell again and held it there.

It had to be Damon! If there was one thing she should have remembered about him, it was his determination to get what he wanted.

He was going to wake Mario up! Her son was a deep sleeper, but he had his limits.

Suddenly anger surged to Abbie's rescue. She wasn't going to hide up here, feeling guilty about the past, because the truth was that it hadn't been her fault. She had been forced to do what she did. And nobody had a right to roll up here and make such a racket at this time of night.

Drawing her dressing gown closely around her slender figure, she marched downstairs, and, taking a deep breath, she threw open the door.

Damon Cyrenci was standing on her porch, leaning against the door jamb with his finger on the bell. Even though she had been expecting to see him it was still a shock.

He stepped back as the door opened, and silence reigned.

For a second his eyes swept over her with audacious scrutiny, taking in everything about her from her bare feet to the wild tumble of blonde curls around her shoulders.

And the strange thing was that for a moment Abbie was transported back to their first meeting, when he had looked at her in exactly the same way. She felt a tug of sexual attraction rising from somewhere very deep inside her. His appearance had hardly altered. The business suit he wore emphasised his fabulously well-honed physique, and the dark thickness of his hair was unchanged. Maybe there were a few silver strands at the temples, but they just made him appear all the more distinguished.

As her eyes held with the dark, searing intensity of his, her heart lurched crazily. He was the same drop-dead-gorgeous man who had stolen her heart away—except that man had only ever been an illusion, she reminded herself fiercely. Despite the heat of the passion they had once shared, she had never meant anything to him. Behind the façade the real Damon had just been a seducer—a predator who'd enjoyed the thrill of the chase and nothing more.

Falling in love with him had been a mistake, and she had learnt her lesson.

The memory helped her to pull herself together and focus her senses.

'Hello, Abigail. It's been a long time.'

His voice was coolly sardonic, and yet the attractive accent still managed to lash against the fragility of her defences.

'What are you doing here, Damon?' Somehow she managed to sound calm and controlled.

'Is that all you can say after all this time?' Again there was the same mocking tone to his question. 'How about "nice to see you, Damon—why don't you come in?"'

The strange thing was that one part of her—the wild, illogical part—wanted to say those words, but his manner forbade it. Something in the cool tone and the glint of his eye told her very clearly that although he was here on her doorstep nothing had changed from their last meeting, and his opinion of her was as low as you could get.

'I haven't got time for games, Damon,' she grated unevenly.

'Really? Strange how you had plenty of time for games in the past.'

Her father's words reverberated through her consciousness. *This is about revenge, Abigail—and you are next on Cyrenci's list.* She swallowed hard and slanted her chin up. 'Obviously this isn't an impromptu social call, so just say whatever it is you've come to say, Damon, and then go. You'll forgive me if I don't invite you in.'

'No—I don't think I will forgive you, Abbie.'

Although he said the words matter-of-factly, there was an undercurrent that struck her and hurt—and that in turn made her angry. Why should he still have the power to hurt her like that? She tightened her hold on the door. 'Well, you are not coming in.'

He shook his head. 'I really don't think you are being very friendly, and I'm sure given the circumstances you can do better than that—in fact, your father assured me that you could.'

What had her father been saying to him? 'I don't know what's been going on between you and my father. I believe you now control the Newland empire—well…' she shrugged '…I don't care. It has nothing to do with me.'

'That's where you are wrong, Abbie. This has everything to do with you.'

The chill certainty in his voice flayed her.

'I just want you to go now.' To Abbie's distress, her voice faltered slightly.

'I'm not going anywhere.'

'Well, you are certainly not coming inside my house.' She started to try and close the door but she didn't move quickly enough, and he put his foot in the way, effectively stopping her.

'Let me spell things out for you a little more clearly.' His voice was suddenly very serious. 'We have unfinished business, and I'm coming in whether you like it or not.'

'Damon, it's late and you're scaring me.'

'Good.' He sounded cold and unyielding.

'I'll have to ring the police if you don't go now,' she threatened shakily.

'By all means, you do that.' For a second his eyes narrowed. 'At least that way we can speed things up.'

'Speed what things up?'

'The legal side of things.' He watched impassively as the colour drained from her face. 'As you have so rightly pointed out, I'm in control of the Newland assets now. And according to company records no rent has been paid on this place for—oh, quite some time.'

'That's because the place belongs to me!' she hissed furiously.

Damon shook his head. 'No, it belongs to me,' he corrected her quietly. 'And I'm here to take stock of my belongings.'

'Well, then, you'd better contact me through my solicitor.'

Damon smiled at that. 'Oh, don't worry, I will be doing that. Because I also want access to my son.'

The words dropped into the silence like a bombshell, and Abbie's limbs suddenly felt as if they didn't belong to her.

'So are we going to do things the easy way or the hard way?' he enquired silkily. 'It's up to you.'

She couldn't answer him. Her hands dropped from the door, and as she momentarily lost her hold on the situation he took his opportunity and walked past her into the house.

His eyes swept over the lounge area, taking in the brown leather sofas, the polished wood floors and the huge stone fireplace. The place was very stylish, but it wasn't what he had been expecting. The furniture, when you looked closely, was old, and everything had a slight air of faded opulence. But Damon wasn't interested in décor; he was searching for telltale signs of something that interested him far more. He found what he was looking for as his eyes lighted on a box of toys by the far end of the sofa, and a discarded teddy bear on a chair. At the sight of those toys his insides knotted with a fierce anger.

'So, where is he?'

As he rounded towards her again, Abbie sensed a seething fury that made her truly afraid. She could hardly think straight for a moment, never mind answer him.

'Where is my son, Abbie? You may as well tell me now, because I will find him even if I have to go through every room in this house—or every house on this island.'

The determination in those words stunned her, but they also brought an inner answering strength welling up inside her. 'You keep away from him, Damon. He is not a belonging listed under the company assets. He is a little person in his own right, and I won't have you marching in here upsetting him.'

'And what about his right to have a father—or doesn't that count in your twisted logic?'

The question smote Abbie's heart. It was something she had asked herself time and time again—something that had kept her awake long into the lonely nights when she had discovered she was pregnant. Yes, she wanted Mario to have a father—a loving father who would put his needs first. But

Damon had left before she'd realised she was pregnant, and she hadn't known where he had gone. She'd tried to track him down, but to no avail. She had consoled herself with the fact that he wouldn't have been interested in his child anyway. Damon didn't go in for commitment, he led a playboy life-style. He'd told her that when they'd first met.

But the strange thing was that when he'd held her in his arms she had imagined that his feelings for her were differ-ent, that what they had shared had meant something. But of course she had been fooling herself. That had been quite clear when he'd walked away from her.

The memory hurt so much that she wanted to tell Damon that the little boy upstairs was not his, and that he had a father in his life—a wonderful, loving father, a man who also loved her. She opened her mouth but the words refused to come.

When it came right down to it, she couldn't lie about some-thing as important as that.

'Of course having a father counts,' she said shakily instead.

'Right—which, of course, is why you came to me and told me you were pregnant?' Damon's tone was scathing.

'And if I had would you have wanted to stay around and play happy families? I don't think so. We had had a few weeks together of wild sex—it meant nothing.' Even as she said the words, the memories that flared inside her made her hot, made her voice tremble with suppressed feeling. 'You said as much yourself—you said…' She shook her head and pulled herself together before the tears could gather in her voice. 'Anyway, all that is in the past and irrelevant. The truth is that I didn't find out I was pregnant until after you'd gone. I didn't know how to get in touch with you. You hadn't left your address or contact numbers. I didn't know where you were.'

'You are good at making excuses.' Damon shook his head. 'No, Abbie, you didn't tell me because your father held the purse strings and you thought I had nothing. That was a more important consideration for you at the time.'

'That's not true!'

'Like hell it's not. You forget, Abbie, that I know you exactly for what you are.' Damon's eyes raked contemptuously over her, but as they did so he couldn't help noticing the sensational curves of her figure beneath the silk of the dressing gown. How come her beauty could still blow his mind? he wondered hazily. How come when he looked at her now after all this time he could still remember exactly how she had felt when he touched her—how she had tasted, how she had moved beneath him?

Back then she had been firm and pert and he had wanted her like crazy—but he could excuse that because he hadn't known the truth about her then.

How come he could feel the same stirrings now?

'We're wasting time,' he grated, furious with himself for being sidetracked even momentarily like this. 'And I've already wasted enough of that.'

To Abbie's horror Damon started to head towards the stairs with a look of determination.

'You can't go up there.' She hurried to stand in his path, tried to grab hold of his arm, but he brushed her away as if she were an annoying fly and swept past her.

'Damon, you have no right!' Her voice caught on a sob as she raced after him, but he didn't break his stride.

'Actually, as the child's father, I think you will find I have lots of rights.'

The words brought a strange kind of helplessness washing over Abbie. It was the same feeling she used to get when dealing with her father. It was the knowledge that someone more powerful than you could dictate your life, and there wasn't anything you could do about it, because if you didn't comply the consequences would be more than you could bear.

She watched as he pushed doors open along the landing into deserted bedrooms.

'Stop it!' The anguished whisper made him halt in his tracks to look back at her.

'Don't bother to try and turn on the false tears, Abbie, because it's not going to work,' he told her acerbically. 'I don't care how you feel—in fact I couldn't give that—' he clicked his fingers softly '—for your emotions.'

'I know,' she said softly. 'I've always known that.'

Something about the way she said those words caught at him, and for a brief second he felt a tug of some long-forgotten emotion as he looked into the blue depths of her eyes. He remembered the first night that they had made love. He remembered the vulnerable way she had looked up at him as she'd allowed him to unfasten the buttons of her dress, almost as if she'd been afraid to trust her emotions to him.

The memory infuriated him. Abbie Newland was an actress—there had been nothing remotely vulnerable about her. She had been playing the part her father had set for her, and she had done it very well, and had enjoyed a little fun along the way.

His dark eyes hardened at the memory. 'Well, at least we understand each other.'

'Yes, at least there's that,' she whispered numbly. 'But you should also understand that my child is more important to me than anything and if you upset him in any way I will make you pay for it.'

She tried to draw herself up as she said the words. It was probably a bit like facing down a lion without any real weapons, but she wanted him to know that she would fight to the death if necessary for her child.

'Just because I don't care about your feelings doesn't mean I don't care about him.'

The answer should have reassured her slightly, but it just stung at raw nerves. Still she held his gaze with determination. 'He's in the room at the far end of the corridor,' she said quietly. 'Let me go into the room first, just in case he's awake. You are a stranger to him. I don't want you scaring him.'

Damon considered her words for a second, and then stepped back to allow her to lead the way.

Her whole body felt as if it were shivering with reaction as she walked past him. She guessed she was in shock.

Why did Damon want to see his son? She couldn't believe it was out of any paternal interest. Those sentiments didn't fit with the man she knew him to be. Maybe this was just curiosity. Maybe he would take one look at his child, make a token pretence of being interested, before getting back into his car to get on with the real things in life that mattered to him, such as revenge and money and power... And, of course, womanizing.

Yes, that was probably what would happen, she told herself as she opened the door to Mario's room.

She was relieved to see that the child was still sleeping. He was lying on his back, his face turned sideways against the pillow. He looked the perfect picture of peaceful innocence, his cherub mouth slightly parted, his long dark lashes resting against the satin-smooth skin.

She glanced back at Damon. 'You can come in, but only for five minutes.'

'I think your days of being in charge of this situation are over, Abbie,' he said quietly as he stepped past her.

The words hit Abbie like a punch to the solar plexus. But the feeling was nothing compared to the reaction she felt, witnessing the powerful intensity on Damon's features as he looked down at his sleeping child.

She felt her heart racing against her chest as the realization hit her that this was about far more than just idle curiosity, and to try and dismiss what was happening in such a way would be to vastly underestimate the situation.

For a long moment Damon just looked at his son. Then abruptly he turned and left the room.

For a second Abbie couldn't move. Her mind was reeling with confusion—she couldn't get a handle on this situation at all. What were Damon's intentions? Why was he really here? Hastily Abbie followed him back out onto the landing.

He was already at the other end of the corridor. 'So, now you've seen him,' she said breathlessly. 'Where do we go from here?'

He made no reply; he didn't even look around at her, just headed down the stairs. The front door was still lying wide open, and he marched through it without closing it behind him.

'Damon, where do we go from here?' she asked again, a note of desperation in her voice. She needed to make some sense of tonight, needed to understand what Damon was think-ing—and she couldn't let him walk away without giving her some clue as to what was to happen next.

'Damon?' She followed him downstairs and out onto the porch. 'Damon, *please*!'

His footsteps slowed and then he looked around. 'That's better.' There was a gleam in his eyes as he looked over at her. 'If you keep that tone in your voice, we just might get some-where.'

The cold churning in the pit of her stomach intensified.

'I agree that we need to talk rationally about this situation.'

He made no reply, and she thought he was going to climb into his car and drive away, but then to her surprise he went to the back of the vehicle and took out a small bag.

With the flick of a switch the car was locked again, and then he was heading back towards her with resolute strides.

Although there was a part of her that was glad he wasn't just going to drive away, leaving her wondering what was going to happen next, she didn't like the look of this latest development at all. Her heart thumped nervously against her ribs. 'Where do you think you are going with that bag?'

'I'm bringing it inside my house,' he said curtly. 'And then I'm going to have a drink and get into bed, because it has been a very long day and I'm tired.'

'You can't stay here!'

'Why not?'

'Because…I don't want you here.'

He stepped past her and into the house. 'Tough.'

The door slammed closed behind him.

CHAPTER THREE

FOR one horrible moment she thought he was going to turn the key in the lock, leaving her stranded outside in the dark in her dressing gown. But to her relief the door opened easily as she turned the handle.

With a mixture of trepidation and fury, she glanced around. His bag was at the base of the stairs and she could hear him opening and closing cupboard doors in the kitchen.

She followed the sounds and watched from the doorway as he found a bottle of vodka and poured himself a drink. 'What are you playing at?'

'I think I just told you.' He lifted the glass in a mocking salute.

With difficulty she reined in her temper. This situation was not going to be resolved by losing her cool.

'Damon, you can't stay here. It's not appropriate.'

He laughed at that. 'As if you'd know anything about appropriate behaviour! I have to say, all those years mixing with the aristocracy at those English boarding schools weren't wasted, were they? You've certainly learnt the art of pretending to be genteel.'

With difficulty she ignored the insult. 'This isn't solving anything. Why don't you go and check into a hotel for tonight and then come back tomorrow? We can talk properly when we have both calmed down and are thinking rationally.'

'I am calm.' He took a sip of his drink and regarded her levelly over the rim of the crystal glass. 'And I'm thinking very rationally. It's one in the morning, there's a storm coming in, and I have no intention of going to a hotel now—especially as I own a perfectly good house here.'

'Damon this is ridiculous!' Her voice rose in panic. 'You are not being at all reasonable.'

One dark eyebrow rose. 'Really? I think given the circumstances I'm being extremely reasonable. Let's look at the facts, shall we? You don't actually own this property. In fact, you are heavily in debt and behind with rent—'

'I am no such thing!'

'Plus you've hidden my child away from me, depriving me of precious time with him,' Damon continued as if she hadn't spoken. 'I don't think any court is going to look too kindly on you at all. In fact, I think you will be the one who is judged unreasonable.'

'You're twisting the facts!' She pushed a distraught hand through her blonde hair. 'I didn't know I was pregnant until after you'd gone. I didn't hide anything. And will you stop pretending that you give a damn about having a child? We both know that you would still have walked away from him even if I'd told you I was pregnant.'

'Do we?' Damon's voice grated with sarcasm. 'You don't know the first thing about what I would have done, because you don't really know the first thing about me.'

'I know that you are a playboy who likes to roam the pleasure fields.'

'Certainly.' He inclined his head. 'And I never planned on having children of my own. But you've changed that.'

Damon looked at her pointedly. 'Enlighten me, Abbie.

What were you planning on telling my son when he gets older? That his father is dead? Or that his father didn't want to know him?'

Abbie hesitated. 'I wouldn't have lied to him. I'd have handled it.'

'Believe me, no matter how you handled it, it still wouldn't have been right.' Damon's voice was heavy. He remembered all too well what it was like growing up without a parent. His mother had walked out of the family home when he was eight. It was so easy to screw up a child's life. Maybe that was why he had avoided settling down and having children. The responsibility was awesome, and he believed implacably that a child deserved two parents and a stable home.

'You had no right to keep Mario a secret from me.' Damon's eyes burnt into hers. 'Any court will tell you that.'

'He wasn't a secret. And will you stop talking about courts and judgements!'

He shrugged and took another sip of his drink. 'Courts and judgements are very much the reality; you better get used to it.'

'Why are you being like this?' The question sprang from her lips with anguish.

'Like what?'

'So…brutal…as if you want to punish me.'

He looked at her then, and gave a short, mirthless laugh. 'Why do you think?'

The sardonic question tore at her. 'My father was right—this is all about revenge, isn't it?' She made herself say the words, her voice trembling with emotion.

He took another sip of his drink, and then threw the remaining contents of the glass down the sink.

'You're angry about what my father did, and I understand that.' Abbie tried very hard to remain calm. 'And I'm sorry for my part in it. But as I tried to explain long ago, it wasn't my fault I—'

'Of course not. But then shallow, spoilt socialites like you don't believe in taking responsibility for your actions, do you? You think you can do what you want, and sorry is just a word.' His voice grated with sarcasm. 'But let me assure you that angry is a bit of an understatement for how I'm feeling right now.'

Abbie glared at him furiously. 'I am none of the things you have accused me of being.'

'And Father Christmas really does slide down chimneys on Christmas Eve.'

The scorn in his voice made Abbie's temper soar. But, as much as she would have loved him to know the truth about the past, she knew she could never tell him about her mother now. She had tried to explain her actions to him at their last meeting. She had braved the contempt in his eyes, and had haltingly started to open up to him, only to have him laugh scornfully in her face and cut her off. She couldn't go through that again. The pain of trying to tell him something so raw, so deeply personal, was beyond endurance. And why should she put herself through that when it was clear his opinion of her hadn't changed? He thought she was a liar, and he wouldn't listen to any explanation—wouldn't believe her, anyway. It all hurt far too much.

Some things were best left in the past, she told herself firmly. What mattered now was her child's welfare.

That fact made her swallow her fury and keep her cool. 'So you want to punish me,' she forced herself to continue. 'I can handle that. But going to a court to get access to a child you don't want—that isn't going to make this right. Please don't take this out on Mario.'

'How do you know I don't want him? You're making sweeping assumptions.' Damon's voice was cool. 'What did you think was going to happen when your father told me I had a child? Did you think I'd just throw money at you and disappear? If that's what you want, then you are dreaming. Because, believe it or not, I'm thinking about what is best for my son now. Something you seem incapable of.'

'I have always put my son first,' Abbie told him fiercely. 'And I don't want anything from you.'

He fixed her with a look that told her in no uncertain terms that he didn't believe her.

She swept an unsteady hand through her hair. Obviously he was never going to believe that she was anything other than a scheming witch. 'So what are you going to do?' she asked quietly. 'What do you consider *best* for Mario?'

Damon didn't answer her immediately. He appeared to be thinking about his options. Abbie could feel her nerves twisting and stretching. Was he deliberately trying to torment her? Was this part of his revenge? Maybe she should be flinging herself on his mercy instead of being confrontational.

But on the other hand maybe that was what he wanted. Her father used to enjoy controlling her through fear. When she'd tried to rebel, he'd reminded her of what he could do, and she would be yanked quickly back into line.

The memory made her angle her chin up defiantly to meet Damon's cool gaze. She had sworn that no one would ever have that power over her again. 'If you go for custody, I'll fight you every step of the way.'

'That's your prerogative.' He shook his head. 'I admire your spirit—but of course I will break it.'

He watched the bright glitter of fury in her eyes. She was so very beautiful—more so than she had been at eighteen; her father had been right about that. The thought stole, unwelcome, into his mind and he found his gaze drifting down once more over her body. He could see the firm curves of her breasts through the thin silk of the gown, and because the bright lights of the lounge were behind her he could also see the long, shapely outline of her legs.

She had always been attractive, but she had matured into a stunningly desirable package. Pity about her cold, mercenary heart, he thought dryly.

Abbie noticed the way he looked at her—noticed, and bizarrely felt her body throb, as if his eyes were actually touching her. She tried to ignore the feeling, tried to pretend it wasn't happening. How could she feel like this when her mind was racing with fear—when she hated him? 'Maybe you just have rage issues that need to be readdressed, Damon,' she said evenly.

He laughed. 'Maybe you are right.' He put his glass down on the draining board with a thud.

'So what are you going to do?'

'Right now, I'm going to bed,' he said calmly.

'You can't!'

'Why not?'

'Because you can't make statements like that and just leave things! I need to know what your intentions are regarding Mario. You are not really thinking of fighting me for custody, are you?'

Damon stared at her for a moment. When John Newland had told him he was a father, he had been shocked—then he had been furious. All kinds of emotions had been racing through him ever since. Some of the feelings had come as a complete surprise to him—such as the feeling of protectiveness when he had looked down at his sleeping child.

Yes, he'd decided a long time ago that he wasn't going to settle down and have children. But the fact was he had a child, and abandoning him wasn't an option. He couldn't walk away from that responsibility; he strongly believed in doing the right thing.

But what *was* the right thing in this situation? His eyes flicked over towards Abbie, and for a second he found himself thinking about her father's words to him in the boardroom.

Abbie could be of use to him.

The words sizzled provocatively through his consciousness. Abruptly he tried to dismiss them. 'I'll sleep on the problem, and we'll discuss terms in the morning,' he grated tersely.

He was so arrogant! So infuriating! She watched as he walked past her towards the lounge.

'I don't want to discuss terms in the morning. I want to discuss terms now! And it may have escaped your notice but there are no spare beds in the house. All the rooms you looked into tonight are empty. The only other bed in the house is mine.'

He turned slowly and looked at her. 'Is that an invitation?'

He watched the flare of heat under the creaminess of her skin with detachment.

'You know it's not.'

'Do I?' He shrugged. 'Nothing you would stoop to would surprise me. In fact, when I faced your father in the boardroom at Newland he made me a very bizarre offer.'

'What kind of an offer?'

'The deal was that I help him retain his place on the board, and in return I get you.'

'What do you mean, you *get* me?' Her voice was stiff.

'Just what I said. In return for my help getting him back on the board of directors, he said he could arrange for you to… Well, accommodate me in whatever way I saw fit, really. I'm not sure if he was selling you as a trophy wife who would have very useful business connections, or the convenient mistress there to entertain me in bed, plus play hostess when required—

that kind of thing. Of course, the second option caught my interest more at first. As you know, I'm not the settling-down type. But then, I didn't know I had a child at that point.'

He watched the colour flooding back into her cheeks. 'Don't worry, I turned him down. My motto has always been to cut out the middleman. Dealing direct is a much more satisfactory solution, don't you think?'

'What I think is that you are just as vile as my father.' Her voice trembled alarmingly. Just when she thought her father couldn't get any lower in her estimation, he sank to new depths. She felt degraded and humiliated by him—soiled by association.

'Dear me, have you had a fall-out with darling Daddy?' Damon walked back towards her and reached out to trail a finger down over the smoothness of her skin. 'What's the matter, are you annoyed because he can't bankroll you anymore?'

She flinched at the touch of his hand. She didn't know what hurt more, her father's disgusting business proposition or Damon's glib acceptance that she would be in any way amenable towards it!

His eyes held with her glittering gaze. 'Never mind. Although I've cut your father out of the equation, I'm still weighing all the possibilities up, I assure you. Trophy wife versus convenient mistress…' He shrugged. 'Or should I just take custody of Mario and walk away… The choices are endless.'

'You wouldn't get custody of Mario,' Abbie told him heatedly. 'And I wouldn't marry you if you were…if you were the last man left on the planet and lived in a gold-plated palace.' She angled her head up proudly.

Damon laughed at that. 'Oh, but we both know that you would.'

'You always did have an inflated opinion of yourself.'

'I just know how Ms Abigail Newland's gold-digging mind works.'

'You know nothing about me. I would rather die than go along with the idea.'

Damon smiled 'You didn't pass away with righteous indignation when you got involved with your father's deals last time.'

He watched her lips part noiselessly, watched the shadows flicker across the beauty of her eyes. 'That was different.'

Damon shook his head. She was a good actress, he'd give her that. 'You go where the money is—your father told me that about you over two years ago.'

He watched as her hands clenched and unclenched at her sides. She had such slender hands. Everything about her was so feminine; even her rage was simmering, contained—lady-like. Although, he remembered that in bed she hadn't been quite so restrained—not once he'd taught her what he liked and how he liked it.

He wished he could stop thinking about that. But the fact was he couldn't.

From the moment she had opened the front door to him tonight, he'd known that sexually he still wanted her.

He wanted her now. The strength of that need totally infuriated him. How could he feel like this when he knew her for what she was—disliked her, even?

He hated that. But it was a fact, and no matter how he kept telling himself to ignore it he couldn't. So what the hell was he going to do about it?

His eyes moved up over her body slowly, appraisingly. He had no doubt in his mind that she had known about her father's offer to him and had been hoping to play it for all it was worth.

Maybe the best thing to do here was to take control and play her at her own game. The more he thought about that idea, the more he liked it.

'So…' His tone was measured, his mind ticking over his options. 'You want to talk terms? Let's talk terms.'

The way he was looking at her was anything but clinical, yet the tone of his voice was detached, objective. What the hell was running through his mind now? Abbie wondered nervously. She moved her hands to draw her gown more tightly around her body, unaware that the instinctively protective gesture only showed her figure to clearer advantage.

She wanted to tell him to get out, that she wouldn't talk to him after the things he had said to her—the things he had insinuated. But she forced herself to calm down and think about what was important. And that was Mario. 'My terms are that my child stays where he belongs, and that's with me. Let's face it, Damon, you are a businessman who jets off around the world at a moment's notice. You sit in meetings that run on until the small hours. That doesn't fit with looking after a twenty-one-month-old baby. He's a full-time commitment.'

'Yes, he is. And that's the one reason I'm prepared to offer you a good deal.'

'What kind of a good deal?' The words were out before she could consider them, and she instantly regretted them as she saw the way his lips curved in a cool smile.

'You see? The Abigail Newland I know is never far away, is she?' he hissed. His eyes swept over her body again with a hard gleam of male appraisal. 'In a nutshell?' He shrugged. 'I guess your father's idea isn't completely off the wall. I suppose you would be a convenient package. You are the mother of my child and we understand each other. And, I have to admit, the whole idea of having a lady in the lounge and a whore in the bedroom does appeal.'

Fury swept through her at those mocking words. 'Well, maybe you'd better put an advert in the paper, because I sure as hell am not interested.' Her eyes flashed fire at him. 'The thought of you laying one finger on me makes me nauseous.'

She would have marched past him and out of the room at that point, but he caught hold of her arm and pulled her back.

'We both know that's not true.' Although his hand was holding her firmly, the touch of his skin against hers was like an electric shock sending weird little darts through her body, intruding on her rational mind—making her tremble deep-down inside.

He was right—it wasn't true. It was a long time since they had made love, but she remembered how much she had liked it—remembered how blissful it was to lose herself to the masterful dominance of his caresses, his kisses.

Why was she thinking like this? She hated him, she reminded herself fiercely. He had just insulted her beyond belief—hurt her beyond belief. Had she no self-respect?

'Let me go.' Her voice was harsh with reaction.

'You haven't heard the terms of the deal yet.'

'I don't want to hear the terms of the deal. I'm not interested.'

'Of course you are.' Damon smiled, but his eyes were singularly lacking in amusement. 'Your father has lost everything, and that means you have lost the goose that lays the golden eggs—you've even lost this place. But I can make everything better again.'

'All I have to do is prostitute myself to you—is that it?' Her voice was raw.

'Actually, as the mother of my child I'm prepared to offer you a better deal than that.' Damon spoke calmly, but his eyes seemed to bore down through hers. 'All you have to do is come back to Sicily with me and play at being the perfect wife and mother. Of course, you will have to share my bed. But in return I'll keep you in the style and comfort that you are used to.'

Abbie stared at him, her heart thundering against her chest. She just couldn't believe what she was hearing, or the fact that he was saying these things to her in such a clinical and calculating fashion.

'You'll have to sign a prenuptial agreement, of course. But as long as you abide by my terms and stay in the marriage you will have everything you want.'

'That's supposed to be a good deal, is it?' Abbie suddenly found her voice, but she was almost spluttering with rage. 'You really think I'd marry you? You've got a high opinion of yourself, haven't you? I don't even *like* you.'

'It's the best deal you are going to get, Abbie. The prenuptial agreement is non-negotiable.'

The harsh tone took her breath away.

'Your arrogance is incredible. You think I'd tie myself into a loveless marriage for…for—?'

'For wealth, security and all the baubles and trappings of luxury you could possibly want?' Damon cut across her dryly. 'Yes, I do. So let's just cut the pretence, shall we?'

'Yes, let's.' Her voice trembled. 'Because the truth is that even for all the money in the world I wouldn't want to share a house with you, never mind a bed. The very thought leaves me cold.'

Damon laughed.

'What is so funny?' She glared at him.

'You are. We both know that there's nothing cold about you. Maybe we don't like each other very much.' He shrugged. 'But we have a certain thing called chemistry. When I touch you, you come alive. Sex was always good between us.'

'As I said, you are the most conceited, arrogant man I have ever—' She broke off as he started to pull her closer.

'What are you doing?' She tried to wrench away from him, but he wouldn't let her go.

'I'm going to kiss you and prove a point.'

'Don't you dare!' Her eyes blazed up into his.

He smiled at her. 'The sooner you accept the fact that I'm calling the shots now, the easier it's going to be all around.'

'I will accept no such thing!'

Her breathing was coming in short, uneven gasps from anger and from the effort of struggling against him.

'You are just making life difficult for yourself.'

'No, you are making my life difficult! But that's what you want, isn't it?'

'No, Abbie, right now that's not what I want.'

There was something husky about those words, something strangely inviting. His gaze moved to her mouth.

And suddenly, as his head moved lower, she stopped struggling. She wanted him to kiss her. It was as if a tidal wave of desire suddenly hit her out of nowhere, flooding her entire body, pulling her under into very dangerous currents.

His lips touched against hers, gentle at first, and then as they tasted her acquiescence they became hard, demanding and brutal. She found herself kissing him back with equal strength, as if she couldn't get enough of him, as if she were intoxicated by his strength, by his passion.

Then suddenly, as she reached up to touch him, he pulled back from her.

She looked up at him, dazed by what had just happened. His gaze moved from her lips, down to the plunging neckline of her robe.

She noticed the look, and was suddenly very aware of the fact that if he reached out with his other hand he could pull her robe down from her shoulders, leaving her naked to his gaze.

For a shocking moment she wanted him to do that! She wanted him to touch her intimately, wanted to melt in against the powerful contours of his body. The feeling of longing overwhelmed her, rendered her helpless.

His dark eyes returned to hold hers, and there was a gleam of satisfaction there. 'You see, Abbie? You don't need to like me to make this *arrangement* work. All you need is to be your hot-blooded self and, of course, the perfect mother for Mario.'

Shame washed through her in waves. Why the hell had she kissed him back like that? *Why?*

She angled her chin up and forced herself to glare at him defiantly. 'I kissed you.' She shrugged. 'So what? Maybe I just wanted to give you a taste of what you are missing when I walk away from…from your offer.'

'Well, well,' he drawled softly. 'You really are—how is it you English say?—a chip off the old block, aren't you? Trouble is that, like your father, you have very little ground for negotiation. I'm not going to up my offer, Abbie. The prenuptial agreement is non-negotiable. You take what's on the table or you walk away.'

Her lips parted in a gasp as she realised he thought she was trying to make him increase his offer to her.

'You really are insufferable.' She grated the words unevenly, furious that he should make such an assumption. 'I'm not remotely interested in your offer, or in you.'

The sensual line of his mouth curved into a smile as his eyes once more moved down over her body, to where her breasts were straining against the satin material. She knew he could see the hardness of her nipples through the thin material, shamefully giving away the fact that even though his hands hadn't touched her she had been totally aroused.

'But you are interested, Abbie, because power and money are powerful aphrodisiacs for you. You want me more than you can say.'

She shook her head. 'I hate you!'

For one wild moment she thought he was going to pull her back into his arms to prove otherwise.

His lips stretched into even more of a mockingly amused smile. 'Of course you do, and you hate my money even more.'

To her relief, he stepped back from her. 'Well, why don't you run along to that bed of yours? That's if you really do want to go up there on your own.'

She didn't need telling twice; she almost fell over herself in her haste to get away. 'And why don't you get out of my house?'

He ignored that, merely smiled. 'Nice talking terms with you,' he called to her as she moved through the lounge towards the stairs. 'Think about my offer, because I'm only going to leave it open until tomorrow. After that, you will be doing all your negotiating with my lawyer. And, believe me, he won't be nearly as accommodating.'

CHAPTER FOUR

ABBIE lay on top of her bed, staring up at the ceiling. Outside the weather was deteriorating; she could hear the wind starting to whistle around the house with an eerie intensity. Strange how she had been so concerned about that this morning. But now even the threat of a hurricane outside wasn't as disturbing as the presence within.

Why had she kissed him like that? The question kept pounding through her senses along with the memory of his offer.

All she had to do was go back to Sicily with him and play at being the perfect wife and mother.

He could go to hell. She turned over and thumped her pillow. How she had ever once believed that he was a decent human being, she didn't know! And as for imagining that she had been in love with him! Well, she must have been out of her mind.

He'd made no attempt whatsoever to leave the house. A little while ago she had heard his footsteps coming up the stairs, and she had stiffened, her heart thundering against her chest. There was no lock on her bedroom door, and if he'd come in…

But he had merely gone into the bathroom next door, and the next moment she had heard the forceful jet of the shower being turned on.

She wasn't sure what would have happened if he'd come into her room. Yes, she hated him, but something really strange happened to her whenever he touched her. He made her lose control of her emotions so easily, turned her into somebody she didn't even recognise. And it had nothing to do with his damn money! Just what it was about him that affected her like that she didn't know. All she knew was that it scared her.

She heard him come out onto the landing again and she sat up straight, listening intently. But he turned away from her room and she heard him opening the linen cupboard at the top of the stairs.

He was obviously going to sleep on the sofa and was helping himself to some sheets and a pillow, making himself at home. But then the house did belong to him now. Every time she thought about that her anger soared.

The stables had been her refuge from the world, her place to run to. They had belonged to her mother, and it had always been understood that upon her death they were to revert to Abbie.

Obviously her father had got there first, and had taken the deeds as security.

Abigail's hands curled into tight fists as she thought about her father and his latest trick. Offering her to Damon as if she were a piece of property that could be traded! It hurt so much.

She took a deep, shuddering breath and told herself that it wasn't exactly out of character. John Newland excelled at using people.

Her parents' marriage had been a sham. Her father had married her mother because she'd been a member of the aristocracy and it had suited his purposes to play on that fact. As for her mother, although she had been a member of the upper classes she had been practically penniless when she'd met John Newland. Death duties had forced her to the brink of bankruptcy; she had been contemplating selling the house in Surrey that had been in the family for generations, and the riding stables in St Lucia, when John Newland had appeared in her life and offered to rescue her.

Her mother should have known better than to accept his proposal of marriage, but at the time she had believed that she loved him. It hadn't taken long, however, before she'd realised that far from being rescued she had been trapped in a loveless marriage, and her house had been lost, sold off to the highest bidder.

John Newland had been a controlling man, a bully and a womaniser. He had used his wife's connections and her name unashamedly, and at the same time he had despised her weakness in tolerating his behaviour.

As the years had gone by the relationship had deteriorated; even the birth of their only child, Abigail, had not softened John Newland. In fact he had grown worse, parading his women in front of his wife, and heaping scorn on her if she dared to complain.

Abbie had been six and they had been living in America when she'd first witnessed the full extent of her father's rage—a rage that could come upon him from nowhere and for no reason.

She had been packed off to boarding school in England afterwards, but she hadn't forgotten the scene that night.

Why her mother had put up with such a controlling husband for so long, she didn't know. It was Abigail who'd persuaded her to leave. On her sixteenth birthday, she had helped her mum pack a few belongings and had fled with her to St Lucia.

They had told John Newland that they were just having a few days' break to celebrate her birthday, but they hadn't gone back. And from there her mother had filed for divorce.

John Newland's rage had been fierce. Nobody crossed him.

Nobody walked away unless he said they could go. But Abigail had stood firm by her mother, and when her mother had started to get sick she had given up her chance of a university education to help her build up the stables so that they weren't in any way financially reliant on her father.

Things might have worked out. The stables had started to pick up. They had been selling rides to tourists and doing quite well. They might finally have been free of John Newland if her mother's illness hadn't been serious. The type of treatment she had needed hadn't come cheap, and they hadn't been able to afford it.

Nothing short of a life-and-death situation would have forced Abigail to go back cap-in-hand to her father. She had hated doing it, but she'd had no choice.

And of course John Newland had loved it. He had agreed to help his ex-wife by flying her back to the States and making sure she had the best medical help, but as usual the price of his rescue had been high. He'd blamed Abigail for the fact that his wife had ever felt strong enough to leave him, and he had set about making her pay for that betrayal over and over again. He had even threatened to withhold the medical care for her mother if Abbie didn't comply with his wishes.

Abbie had been forced to return to him in Vegas—to dance attendance and play along in his deals.

The worst of which had been the deal with Damon Cyrenci.

When her father had found out that she had fallen in love with Damon he'd seemed to take even greater delight in making sure, when it was all over, that Damon knew she had been complicit in his schemes.

Abbie lay back down against the pillow and stared into the darkness of the bedroom.

To be torn between doing the right thing for a dying parent and the man you thought you loved was a situation she would never forget. It had been pure torture, and of course there had been the guilt that if she walked away her mother might die. The guilt for the fact that Abigail had encouraged her mother to leave her father in the first place and, if she hadn't, John Newland would have paid whatever it had taken to get her better. Money had never been the issue.

So she'd been trapped in a situation that had felt strangely as if it was all her fault. However, when she had sat next to her mother's bedside and tried to say this, her mother wouldn't have it. 'I had more happiness in the few years of freedom we had in St Lucia than in my entire married life,' she had said firmly. 'I'm glad I left him.'

But then her mum hadn't known that behind the scenes Abbie was being torn apart.

At first her dates with Damon were chaste. With difficulty she drew back from his kisses, and deliberately kept him at arm's length, not because she didn't want him but because she wanted him too much and it scared her.

And she was right to be scared. Anything that involved her father always had a dangerous price attached. He'd drop little lines over to her: 'make sure you see Damon tonight,' 'make sure he's not back till late'. At first she did as she was told without question—the consequences of defying her father were too bleak to do otherwise.

But as she fell further under Damon's spell she was torn more and more inside. She desperately wanted their relationship to be untainted by the association with her father and his requests. She tried to reason with her father, but he didn't want to listen—in fact he was angry that she dared to question him. He told her that there was a weekend coming up when he wanted Damon out of town with his mind off business. 'Take him to my ranch in Palm Springs,' he ordered lazily. 'Entertain him until I tell you it is OK to come back.'

She knew her father was trying to pull a shady deal on Damon's father, also that he would only get away with it if Damon wasn't around to spot what he was doing. So for the first time ever she refused a direct command. But with just one cancelled cheque, her father reminded her that it wasn't her life that was held in the balance.

She wanted so much to fling herself on Damon's mercy at that point and tell him what was going on. She knew he would have been horrified, but at least he wouldn't have blamed her.

But then what would happen? She couldn't expect him to foot the bills for her mother.

Nor could she expect him to go away with her to Palm Springs. Maybe he would even confront her father. Either of those things meant her mother would suffer.

So she decided it was safer to say nothing, and she did as her father requested, and invited Damon away for the weekend. But Damon wasn't the walkover that her father was expecting. He was a shrewd operator, and brought in a lawyer to help oversee the dealings with her father.

She remembered Damon casually imparting this information as they sat alone, dining at the ranch. She remembered her relief; she felt as if someone had removed a death sentence from her. Everything would be OK, she told herself reassuringly. Damon hadn't allowed himself to be duped, and her father wasn't going to win this time. That knowledge made going into his arms so much sweeter.

She remembered undressing for Damon, and the strong, sure touch of his hands on her body. She remembered the wild passion that took them over. She remembered lying cradled in his arms afterwards, believing that she was deeply in love with him…

What an idiot! She couldn't believe now that she had been so stupid. Damon had only been interested in sex, not in love.

He'd enjoyed the thrill of the conquest—taking her over and over again. There had been no soft words, no promises.

And, as Damon enjoyed taking her that weekend, her father was busy buying off his lawyer.

Everyone, it seemed, could be used and bought. Everyone had a price. That was what men like her father seemed to thrive on, but she hadn't realised Damon was like that.

She wiped fiercely at some tears that dared to spill down her cheeks.

She had made a mistake falling in love with Damon, but the one good thing to come out of it was Mario. And no matter what it took she wasn't going to let Damon take him away from her. She was going to fight him.

She had been three months pregnant when her mother had died. It had been her lowest ebb. But she had proved then that she was made of strong stuff. She had picked herself up and she had fled back to St Lucia.

With her mother's death her father hadn't had the same hold over her, and she had shut him out of her life completely. She had started to build up the business in the riding stables again.

It hadn't been easy. Being a single mum with a struggling business had been tough—but she had managed.

No matter what Damon Cyrenci thought about her, she could look him in the eye and know that she was a hard working, decent person, not the money-grabbing gold-digger that he believed her to be.

But hard work and decency didn't help when you had lost your home to the devil.

The truth was that although she had managed to be self-sufficient she didn't have enough money for lawyers if Damon chose to play rough.

A violent roar of thunder tore through the night, and it seemed to echo the anger that tore through her.

He was probably bluffing, she told herself soothingly. He wouldn't want a baby cramping his style. And as for all that talk of offering her marriage—that was probably a bluff as well. Maybe he was just winding her up.

Maybe she would get up in the morning and find him gone.

Abbie buried her head into the pillow and tried to sleep, but it was impossible.

As the first light of dawn crept into the room it was a relief to get up, throw on a pair of jeans and a T-shirt and go across the corridor to see to Mario.

He was awake, and he smiled at her as she walked in.

'Hello, darling.' She bent to pick him up and he gurgled with delight.

Everything was going to be all right, Abbie told herself as she cuddled her son close. The storm outside seemed to be abating; the sun was starting to come out. As she busied herself with her usual morning routine of dressing Mario, the night before started to feel like a bad dream.

Maybe Damon would be gone this morning.

Holding on to that thought, she crept quietly downstairs, carrying Mario tightly in her arms.

The house was silent. The only sign of Damon was a neatly folded sheet and a pillow at the end of the sofa.

He'd gone. Her heart started to soar with relief until she walked into the kitchen. The back door was open, and Damon's tall, powerful body was silhouetted in the frame as he nonchalantly looked out at the morning.

He turned as he heard her. 'Good morning.' His eyes swept over her slender frame and the child in her arms. 'How did you sleep?'

How did he think she had slept? Anybody would think that this was a normal everyday situation, she thought angrily. Anybody would think that he hadn't issued her with an absurd ultimatum last night that threatened to upturn her whole life.

'I slept just fine, thank you,' she lied. She wasn't going to let him know she had spent the night tossing and turning and worrying. 'I thought you would be gone by now.'

'I don't know what made you think that. I made my intentions pretty clear last night.'

Abbie swallowed hard. She really didn't want to think about his intentions. If last night had been some kind of bizarre wind-up, he was taking it a bit far.

She settled Mario in his high chair, and then moved to organise his breakfast and switch on the kettle. Pointedly she tried to ignore Damon, but it was hard because she was aware that he was watching her every move.

Like her, he was wearing jeans and a T-shirt this morning. The casual look suited him, made him look younger than his thirty-one years.

She wished she didn't find him so attractive…but she did. She wished she could stop herself from darting a glance over at him as she walked past…but she couldn't. And as their eyes connected she found herself thinking about the way he had kissed her last night, the way he had made her want him. Abruptly she looked away from him again.

How could you hate someone yet find yourself drawn to him at the same time? It was a mystery. A mystery she could do without, she told herself angrily as she heated some milk for Mario and opened a packet of coffee. Maybe a strong shot of caffeine would help unscramble her brain.

'It looks like we missed the worst of that storm last night.' Damon shut the kitchen door. 'The weather seems to have settled again.'

She couldn't believe that he was talking about the weather now. 'Great,' she said dryly.

'Yes, it is.' He walked across and hooked a chair with his foot to sit down at the kitchen table. Mario smiled at him, one of his big, beaming smiles that made dimples appear in his cheeks. Damon smiled back and reached across to ruffle his son's dark hair.

'I've phoned the airport, and my private plane will be on standby this afternoon.' He glanced over at Abbie again. 'All restrictions on travel have been lifted.'

Abbie had been trying to spoon ground coffee into a pot, but her hand shook alarmingly at those words and most of it ended up on the counter-top. 'You're leaving!' She swung around to look at him.

'Yes. This afternoon at four o clock.'

So everything he had said to her last night *had* been just a wind-up. Relief surged through her. 'Look, Damon, I know it must have been a shock finding out about Mario the way you did. And a lot of things were said last night in the heat of the moment—'

'Were they?' Damon held her eyes steadily. 'I never say anything I don't mean.'

She frowned. She'd been going to tell him that maybe they could put the past behind them, and that he could see Mario when he wanted, because after all he was his father. But she left the words hanging in the air as she sought clarification. 'But you *are* leaving?'

'Yes, I'm returning home to Sicily, with or without you.'

'With?' There was a horrible silence for a moment as she digested this. 'You mean, you meant all that stuff about— about marrying me and the prenuptial agreement... Everything?'

'Everything.'

Abbie felt her heart bounce crazily against her chest at the look of cool determination in Damon's eyes.

She swallowed hard and turned away from him.

'I'll have a coffee while you're there,' Damon instructed calmly.

She wanted to say 'make your own coffee', but she didn't dare. She just poured the boiling water into the pot and got down some cups.

'You accept my offer and come with me to Sicily today, or I leave on my own and put things into the hands of my legal team. It's up to you.'

The decisive tone stirred up a sizzling kind of fear inside Abbie. She had never felt more out of her depth in all her life, and she just didn't know how to play this. So she kept her back to Damon and pretended to be engrossed in making Mario's breakfast.

Damon watched her as she moved around the kitchen. He'd thought long and hard about this situation last night, and the more he mulled it over the more sense his offer seemed to make. He wanted his son—wanted him with a strength and certainty that had taken him completely by surprise. But he knew he couldn't tear him away from his mother. No matter how much he threatened, that just didn't feel right. A child needed his mother. But he needed a father too.

So what should he do?

Offering Abbie marriage had been truly inspirational.

Mario would have his mother, plus he would have Abbie exactly where he wanted her.

She stretched up to an overhead cupboard, and his eyes drifted over the narrow hand-span of her waist to her bottom, noting its sexy curve in the tight jeans. *And he knew exactly how he wanted her.*

It was lust, of course—but there was an easy remedy for lust. He was going to make Abbie Newland pay in his bed for her gold-digging, deceiving ways, and at the same time he was going to rid himself of this thirst for her by taking her over and over again at his leisure.

'So, what's it to be?' he grated harshly. Now he had made up his mind about what he wanted, he wasn't going to wait around.

'I'll have to consider my options.' She tried to school her voice, rid it of all emotion, but there was a tremor there that she knew he would pick up on.

'You haven't got any options.' Damon smiled calmly. 'I've been looking through your accounts. They make dismal reading.'

'You've done what?' Her glance flew towards the small office that led off the kitchen. She noticed now that the light was on, and her papers were spread out across the desk.

'How dare you look through my private papers?' She swung around to face him.

'There's nothing private from me regarding the business here, Abbie. I own it. The sooner you accept that, the sooner we can move on.'

'I'll accept nothing of the sort.' From somewhere she found a flare of her old fighting spirit. 'I shall be seeking legal advice.'

'And what are you going to pay your legal team with?' he enquired with amusement. 'Washers?'

'I have some rainy-day money,' she told him shakily.

Damon laughed. 'Abbie, it's pouring down so hard that you have been washed away, and you know it.'

Abbie swallowed down on the knot of fear that told her he was right. The little money she had would be no match whatsoever against Damon's might.

'I've offered you a way out. Holding out in the hope that I'm going to increase the terms isn't going to work,' he continued smoothly. 'In fact, if you don't accept today, I will pursue a custody claim for Mario—because let's face it, Abbie, you can't even put a roof over our son's head now. He will be better off in Sicily. I can give him everything you can't—a wonderful education, a comfortable home, a good future.'

'And what about love?' The question broke from her lips in anguish.

Damon regarded her steadily. 'I'll be a good father. You have my word on that.'

'That's so reassuring,' she ground out sarcastically.

'Well, if you are worried come with us. You know my terms.'

'I can't just leave—especially at such short notice! I have the horses to sort out, and responsibilities.'

Damon smiled. Things were turning in his favour; he sensed she was starting to crack. 'I'll employ more staff and a manager, and review the situation at a later date. Believe me, this place can be sorted out in a few hours—money has the advantage of making any situation run smoothly.'

'Don't I know it?' Abbie's voice croaked bitterly. Pitted against Damon's wealth and power, she could possibly lose a custody battle…lose Mario for ever. But the alternative was letting him buy her like an extra member of staff. Her mind whirled around and around, searching for an escape route, but she couldn't find one. Instead his words were playing mockingly through her mind. *You can't even put a roof over our son's head.*

He was right. She'd lost the house and the stables, and there was no way she could fight that. What would she do? Where would she and Mario end up?

Was giving in to Damon now her only option? An overwhelming feeling of powerlessness descended on her as she thought about walking away from the home and the animals she loved. And what about her staff here? What would happen to their jobs? Then there was her beloved horse, Benjo, a three-year-old gelding that she'd rescued from a life of grim abuse. He had stolen her heart away with his trusting eyes and his gentle ways. 'I can't…' Her voice broke with anguish.

Damon's eyes narrowed. She seemed so vulnerable, so fragile. He remembered, when they had first been dating, he had sometimes caught that haunted expression deep in the beauty of her blue eyes. He'd seen it that first day when they'd met by the pool. He'd made some joke about her being a social butterfly, and she had looked at him strangely—almost nervously—a million shadows chasing across the beauty of her expression. It had brought out a feeling in him that he couldn't explain, it had made him want to reel her in and hold her tight. No woman had ever made him feel like that before. What a fool he had been. She'd been the one reeling *him* in. She *had* been just a social butterfly—a devious one at that!

Remembering just how devious brought him firmly to his senses. She had played him for a fool once. He wasn't going to be taken in by her ever again. 'Abbie, I haven't got time for your fake emotional outbursts. I don't know whom you think you are fooling. I can see right through you.'

Abbie slanted her chin up and tried to pull herself together. He was so cold—so ruthless—and she was damned if she was going to give him the pleasure of knowing that he was hurting her.

'Coming back to Sicily with me will be the best thing for our son. He will have both his parents, and all the advantages in life that you wouldn't be able to give him. Plus, I shall put a ring on your finger.' Damon shrugged. 'It's a good deal. I'm prepared to be more than generous to you.'

'And I'm supposed to be grateful?' Abbie's voice trembled with anger. 'The ring you want to put on my finger will mean nothing more than a band of possession.'

Damon conceded the point with a curt nod of his head. 'But a band of possession that will entitle you to certain privileges.'

'In return for certain favours.'

'Favours?' Damon looked amused at the term. 'Oh no, Abbie, that's not how our arrangement will work at all.' He stood up from the table to walk towards her. 'The fact is that you like what I can do for you.'

He stood close to her and reached out a hand to trail it down the side of her face. The caress sent a tremor racing through her entire body—but it was a tremor of desire, not repulsion. A tremor that said he was right, she did like what he could do. And that fact disturbed her deeply.

'We're good together, and what's more now we understand each other.' Damon's tone was matter-of-fact, but his eyes were burning over her body. 'You'll just be my good-time girl, but on a regular basis and on a more honest basis than in the past. I hope we are clear on that?'

'Oh, I think you've made yourself more than crystal clear. But there's nothing *honest* about this,' she said huskily.

'It'll be more honest than what happened between us last time.' Damon tipped her chin up so that he could look into her eyes.

The words hurt her so much. She'd loved him in the past—or *thought* she'd loved him. 'Damon, I didn't have a choice, I—'

'There are always choices in life,' he cut across her firmly.

'Like my choice now, you mean?'

For a second the tremble in her voice stole under his defences. He noticed the shadows in the beauty of her eyes, noticed how they changed from deepest indigo to violet-blue.

'Damon, what happened between us was—'

'What—a regrettable mistake?' Reality swirled in around him. It was amazing how for just a moment she could still get to him. Obviously it was because he still wanted her sexually and that clouded his judgement—that had always been his weakness where she was concerned. His lips twisted wryly. 'I suppose from your point of view you could look at it like that. You made the wrong choice, you backed the wrong horse, Abbie—your father can't bankroll you now. But I can.'

It was strange how his voice was so brutal, yet the touch of his hand as he trailed it down her cheek was so seductively gentle. It sent conflicting signals racing through Abbie's body.

'You forget that I know you. I know how your mind works.' His eyes were on her lips.

She felt a lick of heat stirring through her body, the kind of heat that made her long for him to move closer.

How could she feel like this when she was so appalled by his words? She tried desperately to make herself move away from him—but she couldn't.

'This pretence of yours has gone far enough. Let's just cut to the chase shall we? Have we got a deal?' As he asked the question he grazed his thumb over the softness of her lips. The caress made the longing inside her grow stronger. She wanted him to kiss her, to hold her...

She couldn't understand it. How was he able to turn her on like this? How could he make her ache inside with this deep, burning anguish? Of all the men in the world, why *him*?

'Abbie, have we got a deal?' His voice was insistent, and as he spoke he moved his other hand to her waist, pulling her a little closer. She could feel the heat of his body only centimetres away from hers, and the touch of his hand at her waist was like a sharp brand of ownership.

She imagined being owned by him, sleeping with him in the deep comfort of a double bed every night. Her eyes closed on a wave of weakness as she imagined his hands on her body, his lips crushing against hers.

Sex had been so wonderful with him. He was right, there was chemistry between them. And she did like what he could do to her, liked it so much. That fact made her ashamed of herself. But, as much as she despised herself, she wanted him.

'Abbie?'

Weakness was flooding her body; she felt trapped by her circumstances—but also by her own emotions.

'Abbie, have we got a deal, yes or no?'

She shook her head against the deluge of longing that threatened to overwhelm her. She couldn't tie herself to a man who didn't love her.

But what choice did she have?

The question brought back some semblance of sanity. Her eyes flickered open. All she could do now was some damage limitation. 'What about the staff here?'

Damon frowned That wasn't the kind of question he'd expected from her. 'Their jobs will be safe.'

'And I need to read the contract you want me to sign before I can agree to anything.'

She was like a fish emerging from the water, wriggling on the end of a line. Damon's lips curved. 'Ah, at last, the real Abigail Newland!'

'Don't be smart with me, Damon.'

'The contract will state that financially the world is your oyster, just as long as you stay with me and abide by my terms.' Their eyes met and held. 'And you already know my terms.' He enunciated the words clearly. 'So, I'll ask the question for the last time: have we got a deal?'

Her heart was thundering against her chest so hard that it felt as if it were filling the room with sound. There was nothing she could do. He had her exactly where he wanted her, and he knew it. 'Ok…' She shrugged wearily. 'Yes, we've got a deal.'

She saw the flicker of triumph in his dark eyes. 'At last, an end to the pretence.'

CHAPTER FIVE

THE door of the aircraft slammed shut with all the finality of a cell door closing behind her.

Abbie shut her eyes and told herself that she was being fanciful. If she was going to prison, it would be a very luxurious one. It would be a place where her son would be given a good education and a wonderful life.

She was doing the right thing for Mario. She couldn't have fought against all of Damon's might and power. The one thing she had learnt from the years with her father was that if you had a plentiful supply of money it bought you anything you wanted…even people.

And now she had allowed Damon to purchase her.

But what else could she have done?

She still felt a bit dazed from the speed everything had moved at. One moment she had been standing close to him in the kitchen, the next she had been sent upstairs to pack her things.

'Just bring what you can fit in a small suitcase,' he had ordered. 'Essentials to tide you and Mario over. Everything else can be replaced by new things when we get home.'

Home?

Would she ever feel that Damon's house was her home?

Somehow she didn't think so. And she didn't want new belongings. She wanted her old things. She wanted to feel safe. She wanted to feel like she had her integrity back.

But she had the horrible feeling that her integrity had been left behind in her house along with all the belongings she had once cherished.

She could try to make herself feel better by remembering that she had no choice but to accept Damon's terms—which she hadn't. *But that didn't excuse the fact that she had liked the way he'd touched her—had wanted him to draw her closer—kiss her, caress her.*

The aircraft engines roared and Mario wriggled on her lap. She held him close. 'It's OK, baby, there's nothing to worry about,' she whispered soothingly against his ear.

Liar. There is everything to worry about, she mocked herself.

As the aircraft thundered down the runway she could think of a million worries. And number one on the list was how she was going to give herself in marriage to a man who was going to use her purely for sex.

She remembered how he had sought her out when he had discovered her deception in Vegas. How he'd refused to listen to anything she'd had to say. And then, as his rage had died, the coldness and the clarity in his voice as he'd told her the truth of how he had really felt about her all along. *'As far as I was concerned, our time together was all about sex—I felt nothing for you, other than the pleasure of taking your body. Nothing at all.'*

Those words had never left her. She wished they still didn't hurt. She wished she could forget them—*especially now*.

What future happiness could there be for her with a man who just wanted to possess her body and cared nothing for her?

Had she made the worst mistake of her life in accepting his terms now and getting on this plane?

The aircraft left the ground and soared away from the island of St Lucia. If she looked down she might be able to see her house nestled by the palm-fringed bay. She might be able to see her horse galloping out in the paddock, or Jess taking a group of holidaymakers down to the beach for a long ride across the sands.

Life would go on there without her. Whether she had made a mistake or not, she was on the path to a new life now.

She opened her eyes, and her gaze connected with Damon's.

He was watching her with a cool detachment that made her heart start to beat unevenly. Hastily she looked away from him again.

Where would she be sleeping when they arrived at his house? Would he expect her to just move straight into his bedroom?

The question tormented her.

It was two and a half years since their weeks of wild, abandoned passion. But she could still remember it like yesterday. Could remember the way he had made her feel—as if she'd come alive for the first time. And afterwards being held by him had been the most wonderful sensation. She had felt cherished and protected, and he'd made the loneliness deep inside her melt away.

Of course those feelings had just been an illusion, she reminded herself angrily. But, even so, in the intervening years she had failed to find them again. In fact, dates with other men had failed to stir any spark of excitement inside her. She had wondered if perhaps that side of her was dead. If it had been extinguished by the pain and the fear that if she got too close to someone she might be hurt all over again.

And then Damon Cyrenci had walked in through her front

door and had blown all those theories to smithereens. He could turn her on with just a glance.

It was a cruel twist of irony that the man who had smashed her heart, the man who cared nothing for her feelings—who despised her, even—was the one man who could turn her on.

She couldn't sleep with him tonight, she just couldn't. Fear shot through her in violent waves. She didn't know what frightened her most: the fact that she wanted him so much, or the fact that once he took her to bed she would reveal just how vulnerable she was where he was concerned. He already had such a powerful hold on her; giving him the satisfaction of knowing he was right, and she was his for the taking any time he pleased, was more than her pride could bear.

The aircraft levelled out and the seat-belt sign was switched off.

'Do you want a drink?' Damon stood up and headed to the back of the plane.

'No, I'm all right, thank you.'

She watched as he poured himself a coffee in the galley kitchen, and she tried to direct her thoughts away from what was going to happen between them. This was a lengthy overnight flight. They wouldn't be landing in Sicily until the early hours of the morning. The sleeping arrangements were a long way off.

She glanced away from him around the interior of the plane. She had never been in a private jet before. The last flight she had taken had been a scheduled one from Vegas when she had fled from her father. That flight had been full, and the seats had been jammed close together.

By contrast they were alone on this flight. The deep leather seats were soft and luxurious and placed far apart. There were personal TV screens that could be pulled down from the ceiling above her, and phones concealed in the armrests. There was also a recline button that would fully adjust and transform the chair into a bed.

Damon returned to sit opposite her. 'Do you want to put Mario down on the seat next to you?' he asked. 'Now that we are airborne it might be more comfortable. There is a booster seat, and you can put a blanket and the safety belt around him.'

'Thank you, Damon, but we're fine,' she assured him stiffly. Somehow she didn't want to relinquish the warm little body close to hers.

'Please yourself.' Damon shrugged and reached for some papers in the central armrest. 'I have some work to do,' he murmured.

Abbie looked out the window. How could he be so relaxed about this situation? How could he study his sheets of figures and concentrate on high finance when he had ridden rough-shod over her, made her homeless, torn her away from every-thing she knew?

Because he didn't care, she thought tiredly. Retribution was all he cared about.

Abbie leaned her head back and closed her eyes. Somehow she would get through this, she told herself fiercely. She had to, for Mario's sake.

Silence fell between them, filled only by the drone of the aircraft and the rustle of his papers.

Damon didn't look up from his work until a few hours later, when Mario made it known that he was hungry.

He watched as she soothed the child and moved him into the seat beside her.

She was good with him, he thought, as he watched Mario smile at her suddenly.

But then Abbie could charm the birds off the trees.

His eyes moved down over her figure. She was wearing the jeans she'd had on this morning, but she'd changed her T-shirt for a clinging black top with spaghetti straps. It kept riding up at her waist as she bent to secure Mario in his seat. Her skin was firm, and tanned a golden honey. Her hair swung silkily around her shoulders as she moved.

How he itched to take her; the need for her was burning him up inside. When he'd pulled her close to him in the kitchen this morning he'd wanted to unfasten those jeans and pull off her T-shirt to reveal the soft swell of her curves. And it would have been so easy to have her there and then. He'd seen the flame of desire in her eyes—a flame she had desperately tried to hide behind the pretence of being hurt by the crudeness of his offer.

'OK, sweetheart, dinner is coming.' She bent close and kissed the child. Then she glanced over at Damon. 'Watch him for me, will you, while I heat him something up?'

'Sure.' He inclined his head. Oh yes, she was sweetness personified—nobody would ever guess that her only qualm about selling herself to him had been how good a deal she would get from him.

Well, as soon as she signed his prenuptial agreement her game would be over and his would just have begun.

He put his papers to one side and reached to pick up one of Mario's toys that had fallen on the floor. He smiled at the child as he handed it back. Mario smiled back at him.

Pleasure intensified inside Damon. Oh yes, things couldn't be better. He had his son, and this was all working out very well.

Abbie returned a few moments later, and knelt down beside the little boy to help him with his dinner. Darkness fell outside the windows. Damon returned his attention to his work. He had a backlog to deal with, and he wanted to be sufficiently up to date when he returned to Sicily to be able to take some time off—time that he intended to spend making up for lost time with his son, and enjoying himself with his newly acquired wife…over and over again.

The sun was rising slowly in the east when Damon finally put his work away and the private jet started to make its final descent. Abbie leaned forward and watched as they skimmed in low over the Mediterranean. She noticed the golden glitter of sun on the water beneath them, and the dark shapes of fishing boats. As they approached the land she could see cypress trees and steep mountains silhouetted against the pink of the morning sky.

The touch-down was smooth, and within a few moments they had taxied to a halt and the seat-belt sign was switched off.

They were on the island of Sicily. Abbie wondered if she would suddenly wake up and find herself back in her own bed, find the last twenty-four hours had all been a wild figment of her imagination.

But as she turned her attention back inside the plane and her eyes met with Damon's she knew that this was real. There was no peace of mind to be found. Her future started here.

'Home sweet home.' His lips curved in a slightly mocking smile, as if he could read her consternation.

'If you say so.'

His smile merely widened at that. 'At least we are off to a good start.'

She looked at him enquiringly.

'You realise that what I say goes.'

'Very funny, Damon.'

'Who's joking?' He flicked her a wry look before standing up to gather their belongings from the overhead locker.

She angled her chin up and forced herself not to give him the pleasure of knowing that she could feel every nerve-ending inside her stretching and shaking under the tension.

The door of the aircraft slid open, and Abbie picked up her bag and gathered Mario up into her arms. It was a pleasure to step outside. The morning air was fresh with the promise of a hot day to come, and as Abbie followed Damon down the steps towards the tarmac she took deep breaths as if she were emerging for the last time into freedom.

There was a group of authorities waiting for them by the base of the steps, and behind them a uniformed chauffeur stood patiently next to a stretch limousine, the passenger doors open, ready for them.

'I need both your passports, Abbie.' Damon held out his hand and she scrabbled in her bag to find them and hand them over.

As the formalities of customs and immigration were observed smoothly and within minutes, it suddenly struck Abbie that this was a way of life for Damon Cyrenci.

He was used to people treating him with respect—used to his path being eased, to getting everything he wanted. She noticed their luggage being efficiently loaded straight into the boot of the waiting limousine.

She had to admit it was impressive, as were the warm tones of his accent as he spoke in his native tongue. It was the first time she had heard him speak in his own language, and she liked it. It gave her a strange, liquid feeling in her bones. The trouble was that it was a feeling that annoyed her intensely.

She didn't want him to have that effect on her, because that was giving him power over her, and Damon had enough power. He was arrogant and insufferable, and she wasn't going to be a walkover for him—no matter how attractive she found him. Maybe everyone else bowed and scraped to him, but she wasn't going to. Pride was the only thing she had left now, and she was going to hold on to it at all costs.

Trying to keep that thought firmly to the forefront of her mind, she walked across towards the waiting car.

A few minutes later they were speeding away across the tarmac, out of the terminal and onto the main road.

Damon talked to the driver in Italian for a few moments before closing the glass partition. 'Won't be long, and we'll be home.'

Abbie turned away from him and tried to pretend that she was interested in the scenery. 'You've still got our passports,' she reminded him curtly.

'They are with the rest of the documentation.' He stretched his long legs out. 'I don't know about you, but I could do with a shower and a lie down.'

His words prickled against her senses. Would he expect her to 'lie down' with *him*? 'They say the best cure for jet lag is to stay awake as long as possible, and try to sleep at the normal time,' she told him stiffly.

'Do they?' She could hear the underlying amusement in his tone. 'We'll have to try and think of a way to keep awake, then.'

Abbie bit down on the softness of her lower lip and kept her gaze averted from him. She watched as the Sicilian countryside flashed by in a whirl of colours. She noticed the baked, hard terracotta soil, the silver green of olive trees and the fierce blue of the sky. But all she could think about was the sleeping arrangements at the end of their journey.

The driver turned the car up through the winding, mountainous roads before dropping them back down towards dazzling views out across the coastline.

Then they slowed down and turned into a hidden entrance. Electric gates wound back to allow access to a long driveway that wound its way through lush Mediterranean gardens. As it curved around, Abbie had her first glimpse of the place that was to be her new home.

Her lips parted in a gasp of admiration, for it was more beautiful than she had ever imagined. It had the size and grandeur of a mansion, but it also had a character that stole her heart away.

Vines tangled across the warmth of the red bricks, jasmine and bougainvillea vying for position over the elegant arch of the front door.

'This is a beautiful house, Damon.' Despite the fact that she had been determined to make no comment about her surroundings, her enthusiasm would not be curbed, and it broke from her lips before she could check it.

'I'm glad you approve.' By contrast, Damon's voice was dry. It was as if he had expected her admiration, which of course she supposed he had. After all, his home had all the trappings associated with the residence of a multimillionaire: an infinity swimming-pool sparkled and merged into the deep, hazy blue of the Mediterranean, tennis courts were towards the other side and vast lawns sprawled out at the front.

As the car pulled to a halt by the front door a slim, smartly dressed woman in her late fifties stepped out of the house to greet them. She had dark hair swept into a chignon, and high cheekbones that gave her a regal air.

'This is my housekeeper, Elise,' Damon informed her as he climbed out into the heat of the day. 'Elise speaks good English, is a great cook and runs the house very efficiently. So there will be no problems for you to deal with.'

Abbie frowned. In St Lucia her days had been packed—she had worked long hours, and sometimes it had been difficult juggling motherhood and running the business. There had been days when she had longed for some time and space just to be able to spend time with Mario. But she had also enjoyed the challenge.

How would she fill her days here? she wondered.

Elise welcomed her with a friendly smile, and then cooed and fussed over Mario in Italian.

They stepped into the entrance hall where a grand, curving staircase led up to a galleried landing.

'I have a few business calls to make, Abbie,' Damon informed her curtly as the chauffeur carried in their bags. 'Elise will show you up to the bedroom. Go and make yourself at home. I'll be up presently.'

Abbie's heart was starting to thud so hard against her chest that it hurt. It sounded like he was ordering her to go upstairs and prepare for him!

Maybe he imagined, because she'd agreed to his terms, that all he had to do now was snap his fingers and do as he pleased with her. Well, he could think again. She had far too much self-respect to allow him to use her like that.

Oh no, Damon Cyrenci, you are not getting everything your own way, she told herself fiercely as she followed Elise up the staircase. She may have agreed to his obnoxious terms, but it didn't mean she was going to be a complete pushover.

The room Elise showed her into was palatial. Two arched windows allowed sunlight to flood in. One looked out towards the glitter of the pool and the sea, the other looked over the side gardens. But it was the bed that took her attention. It was a massive king-sized four-poster swathed in white, and it totally dominated the centre of the room.

'There is a dressing room through here.' Elise opened another door. 'I have placed Mario's cot in here, as Signor Cyrenci instructed.'

Abbie followed the woman and glanced into the room. Sure enough, a large cot was placed next to some walk-in wardrobes. Damon had been busy. All those phone calls before they'd left St Lucia had obviously paid off.

But then, as Damon had said, when you had money the way was smoothed very easily.

She felt suddenly exhausted.

'And there is an *en-suite* bathroom through here.' Elise opened the door next to the dressing room. 'Now, is there anything else I can get for you, Ms Newland?'

Abbie shook her head. 'No, everything is fine, thank you.'

With a nod, the woman took her leave. Abbie sank down onto the side of the bed and put Mario down beside her.

The little boy was delighted to be free, and he pulled himself up and toddled off to explore. She allowed him to run unhindered across the soft white carpet; there was nowhere for him to go, nothing for him to harm himself on, and the freedom was probably just what he needed after being confined for so long.

But what freedom was she going to have now? Obviously Damon didn't expect her to do any housework, which meant she would have no say in the running of the house. Was her only role to be that of mother and bedmate?

She noticed the long bank of wardrobes against the far wall. If she opened them up, would she find Damon's clothes hanging inside? Was this his bedroom? It was hard to tell from just glancing around; there were no personal items on the dressing table or on the bedside tables, not even a book or a clock.

Mario toddled back towards her, and she swept him up into her arms. She didn't have the energy to investigate or even think about this situation any longer. She would bath Mario, have a shower herself and deal with everything else a step at a time.

It took Damon a while to sort out the paperwork in his office. He read through the prenuptial agreement that he had asked his lawyer to draw up. He'd done a good job. Satisfied that everything was in order, he pushed his chair back from his desk and went in search of his quarry.

But when Damon stepped into the bedroom he found Abbie lying on top of the bed, fast asleep. He glanced through into the adjoining room and saw that Mario was also sleeping in his cot.

So much for getting her to sign his contract straight away! He crossed the room and sat down beside her on the edge of the bed. She didn't stir. She was lying on her side, her long, blonde hair slightly obscuring her face in a silky curtain. His eyes travelled down over her body, noting the fact that she'd changed into a white pencil-skirt, a white short-sleeved top and that her long legs were bare.

She looked achingly beautiful. He reached out a hand and stroked a strand of her hair back from her face. She moved a little at his touch but she didn't wake.

It was hard to believe that someone who looked like her had such a cold, mercenary heart. Hard to believe that the only thing that really turned her on was money.

He felt a dull ache of something swirling inside him. She looked so innocent in sleep, almost virginal, her lips parted softly, and her long, dark eyelashes thick and sooty against the soft perfection of her skin.

He remembered how he had felt when he had discovered that she was complicit in his father's destruction. She had played the game so perfectly—luring him in, drawing back from his kisses as if scared by the intensity of passion that had sprung between them, teasing him with her tremulous smile and her innocent, big blue eyes. But all the time she had known exactly what she was doing.

There was nothing innocent about Abbie. The knowledge stabbed through him fiercely as his eyes travelled lower over the soft curves of her body. She knew exactly how to use that beautiful body of hers to maximum effect. Knew exactly what she wanted.

Well, so be it—she could use her beautiful body to full effect, she could even have everything she wanted...but at a price. Their roles had been reversed. The huntress was now the prey. He was in control this time.

'Abbie.' He stroked a hand down over her face. 'Abbie, wake up.'

Her eyes flickered open. She looked disorientated for a moment, as if she didn't know where she was. And as she looked up at him the intensity of her kitten-blue eyes seemed to mock his determination to be cool and ruthlessly in control.

'So much for staying awake,' he said softly.

'I only meant to rest my eyes for a moment.' She stretched sleepily and his eyes followed the lissome movement. He noticed how she was very clever at showing her body to full advantage. The round-necked top was in a silky material that emphasised the curve of her breasts in a tantalizingly provocative way, especially when she put her hands over her head like that. The skirt showed how tiny her waist was, and how curvy her hips.

'Good job I've come to your rescue and woken you up,' he grated sardonically. 'We don't want jet lag interfering with our fun, do we?'

As sleep faded from Abbie's mind, the realization of her situation flooded back in. How long had Damon been in the room? How long had he been sitting beside her, watching her sleep?

She drew herself up. 'Damon, what are you doing in my room?'

'Your room?' His lips twisted with amusement. 'This is *our* room, Abigail. This is our marital bed.'

'Well, we are not married yet!'

Although her eyes flared with fire, she sounded flustered—almost nervous—and he laughed at that. 'Such old-fashioned virtue from such a modern—shall we say to be kind, less than virtuous—woman.'

'When were you last kind where I'm concerned?' she croaked huskily.

'Dear me, are you panicking already about how generous I intend to be?' He looked at her with a raised eyebrow. 'Now I understand the reason for the display of innocent virtuosity.'

He watched as the pallor of her skin flooded with colour. He had to hand it to her, she was a superb actress. 'Don't worry, I will be kind, you will get everything your heart desires.'

He reached out a hand to trail one finger down over her cheek. She flinched away from his touch. 'I don't want anything from you, Damon.' She was smarting from his words, from the touch of his hand. She knew his opinion of her, and it shouldn't hurt so much—but strangely it did.

'Drop the pretence, Abbie—we're past that now.'

The mocking tones lashed across her. She swallowed hard.

There was the sound of a car pulling up outside, and Damon stood up from the bed to go over towards the window. 'Ah, right on schedule. Put your shoes on, Abbie, and come downstairs. We may as well get business out of the way now.'

'I can't leave Mario. He might wake up and need me.' Abbie swung her legs off the bed. She didn't want to go anywhere with him—in fact all she wanted right now was to run away.

'Mario will be fine. There is a child-monitor installed. Switch it on and we'll hear him in my study if he cries.'

'You've thought of everything, haven't you?'

'I hope so.' He moved towards the door decisively. 'Don't be long. I'll be waiting for you downstairs.'

There was no alternative but to do as she was told, so she slipped on her high heels and went to check on Mario.

She tried to tell herself that dealing with Damon in the study was preferable to dealing with Damon in the bedroom. But somehow it wasn't much of a reassurance, and her feelings of vulnerability only intensified as she went down to join him. If it hadn't been for Mario, she might have been tempted to keep on going, out through the front door. But, even with Mario in her arms, where would she go? She had no money and no passport.

The knowledge made her heart thump unevenly as she found Damon's study.

'You've still got our passports,' she reminded him as soon as she entered the room.

'Have I?' He was sitting behind a large desk, flicking through papers, and he barely glanced up.

'You know you do.'

Damon shrugged. 'Well, they are not going to be a lot of use to you now anyway. Why do you want them?'

The calm question disconcerted her. 'Because I just do! You can't keep me prisoner here!'

He laughed at that. 'I've no intention of keeping you prisoner here, Abbie.' He sat back in his chair and opened up a drawer to take out some keys. 'In fact, these are for you.'

'What are they for?'

'One is the front-door key to this house and the other is the key for the brand-new silver-blue sportscar waiting outside on the drive for you. It's just been delivered.'

'Oh!' She was taken aback by the gift.

'Oh indeed.' He smiled. 'You see, I do intend to be generous, and you can come and go as you please. As long as you're here for me when I need you.'

The words were said in a certain, seductive way that made

her heart start to hammer even more fiercely against her chest. She noticed the way his eyes slipped down over her figure— assessing, warm.

'Have a look out the window if you want. You'll be able to see the car from here.' He leaned back further in his chair and watched her lazily. He was curious to see her reaction.

Her hands curled into tight fists at her sides. He was treating her like the mercenary little gold-digger he thought she was, and she wasn't going to play. 'I don't want your damn car,' she told him tightly.

'Abbie, don't be coy, it doesn't suit you and it doesn't fool me.'

'I want the passports back.'

He shrugged. 'And you can have them. But they will be utterly useless. They are out of date.'

'No, they're not!' She stared at him mutinously. 'They have years left on them—'

'Abbie,' he cut across her crisply. 'Mario's passport says that he is Mario Newland. That is not his name. His name is Mario Cyrenci. The error will be made right as soon as possible.'

Damon watched impassively as shadows flickered across Abbie's eyes. 'And, as for you…' He smiled coolly. 'I've arranged for a special licence. We will be married tomorrow afternoon.'

'Tomorrow!' Her eyes widened, and the panic inside her intensified. She felt as if she was backed into a corner with no way out. 'Isn't this all a little rushed?'

'Why wait around?' He leaned forward in his chair. 'All you have to do is sign this.' He tapped the papers that were lying on the desk. 'And then you can have these.' He picked up the keys and dangled them.

'Is this the carrot-and-stick approach?' She tried to make a joke, but her voice rasped huskily.

He smiled. 'You could call it that. And, speaking of carrots…' He picked up a small box from beside the papers. 'I suppose you should also have this.'

He opened the lid, and a magnificent diamond-solitaire ring blazed fiercely as the light caught it.

'You don't need to worry—despite the fact that it's an antique, it's worth a lot of money. It's flawless, and it's set in platinum.'

Abbie swallowed down on the shaft of pain inside her 'Why do you want to think the absolute worst of me?' The trembling question broke from her lips involuntarily.

'You know why.'

She wished he knew the truth—wished she could make him believe that what had happened wasn't her fault. 'Damon, I am not a mercenary person. I had no choice but to go along with my father…' Her voice was full of emotion as she tried to reach him. It was so painful even thinking about the past and her mother. 'I—'

'Save it Abbie,' he cut across her ruthlessly. 'I don't want to hear your excuses. Because only a fool doesn't learn by their mistakes, and I'm no fool.'

She stared at him wordlessly. You couldn't make someone believe you when they were just determined to think the worst.

'Now, are you going to sign these so we can move on?' He picked up a pen and tapped the documents in front of him.

What would happen if she said no? Abbie wondered suddenly. Would she be put back on a plane—without Mario? And a plane to where? She had nowhere to go, and nothing except for the one small suitcase she had brought with her.

'I never sign anything without reading it.' She tilted her chin up proudly. She was damned if she was going to make this easy for him. She wouldn't let him see she was beaten. 'You'll have to leave it with me for a few hours.'

'Fine.' He drummed his fingers on the desk impatiently. Then he picked the ring up out of the box. 'In the meantime, in an act of good faith, should I slip this onto your finger?'

She hesitated, and then shrugged. 'I suppose you could. I can always take it off again.'

Damon's dark eyes gleamed with a moment's annoyance. Every time he thought he had her just where he wanted her, she managed to do some kind of sidestep. 'I've really had enough of your games, Abbie.' He stood up and walked around towards her with a purposeful look in his eye, a look that made her heart race. Then he reached to take her hand in his and slip the ring firmly into place.

It fitted perfectly.

'There.' Instead of letting go of her hand, he sat down on the desk behind him and drew her closer.

'Now, you've had some tokens of my intentions. I think it's time I had some token from you.' He said the words roughly, but bizarrely there was nothing rough about the way his fingers stroked over her hand.

'What kind of a token?' She pretended not to know what he meant—but she understood all too well. She could hear what he wanted in the deep rasp of his voice, see it in the dark flame of his eyes.

'I think you should undress for me, Abbie, and show me exactly what *you* can offer *me…*'

CHAPTER SIX

THE command sent a strange pang of emotion shooting through her. There was a part of her that was horrified by his words, and another part... Well, the other part was weakened by the fact that he had pulled her very close and one hand had moved to her waist. He was so close to her and she could feel the heat of his body, smell the familiar scent of his cologne.

His eyes were dark and commanding as they held hers. Then they moved down towards her lips, and she felt something inside her turn over.

This was the father of her child—the man she had loved so passionately once, the man who had made her cry with pleasure when he'd brought her to climax. The man who had chased away the loneliness inside her and held her so tightly against him that she'd thought she would die from happiness.

The memories swamped her, just as they did every time he came too close.

She didn't want to feel like this. But somehow she just couldn't help herself.

'Don't, Damon.' She whispered the words unsteadily.

'Don't what?' He reached up to stroke a stray strand of hair away from her face.

The strangely gentle caress was like pure torture. 'Don't torment me!'

His eyes gleamed with a moment's dark humour. 'Darling Abbie,' he grated sarcastically. 'Why should I listen to that plea when you torment me so well?'

'Do I?' She looked into his eyes, startled by the remark, and he laughed.

'You know, if they were handing out Oscars for this performance you'd get one. You play innocent so damn well.' His words rasped with a slightly uneven edge.

'Now you're mocking me!' Her eyes clouded.

'Now you're going for the "best actress" award as well as "best newcomer".'

'Leave me alone, Damon. I'm not going to allow you to insult me like this—I deserve better!'

'Really?' His tone was sardonic. 'Well, show me what you think you deserve, then.' He let go of her suddenly.

The challenge riled her—riled her almost as much as the fact that he wasn't holding her now. She wanted to feel his arms around her.

She frowned as the realization struck. She wanted him to treat her the way he had when they were lovers; even if it was just an illusion of love, it was better than nothing.

She shut her eyes and leaned closer, and before she could think better of her actions she kissed him. It was gentle at first, almost tentative, but as she felt the warmth of his lips moving against hers she deepened the kiss. For a while she was in control, and she liked it—liked the feel of his body against hers, liked the way he responded to her.

Memories licked through her body, heating her up, making her ache. There had been this tenderness between them in the past, this tentative yet highly inflaming spark. She could feel it now, burning against her lips, sizzling through her consciousness.

His hands were on her waist again, drawing her closer. She could feel his arousal pressing against her.

She wanted him…wanted him so much.

His hands swept upwards and over her breast, caressing her gently, finding the hard peaks of her nipples and stroking them, teasing them into tight, throbbing buds that strained against the satin of her clothing.

'Now, this is better…' His words cut through the warmth inside her.

She closed her eyes and strove to cut the cynical tones from her mind. 'Damon, we were so good together once.' She whispered the words huskily. 'Maybe we could be like that again.'

When he didn't answer, she pulled away from him a little so that she could look into his eyes. 'Maybe we could put the clock back to the way we were together that weekend in Palm Springs?'

'When I didn't know the truth about you?' His eyes held hers steadily. 'I don't think so, Abbie.'

The sudden coldness in his tone struck her uncomfortably.

'I just thought… We have a child together, and if we are going to make this…situation work, then maybe we should try to forget the past.'

'Nice thought.'

Still the coldness was there in his tone.

'At least we could meet each other half way?' She looked up at him with beseeching blue eyes.

'And after we've met half way—then what?'

'Well, I told you, we could put the clock back, start again.'

'Just like that?' He snapped his fingers.

'We could, if it was what we both wanted.' Her heart was thundering against her chest. 'And it would be better for Mario if there wasn't this tension between us, if we could trust each other.'

He didn't answer her immediately, but his hands dropped completely away from her, leaving her aching for him.

'Well go on, then, show me how much you mean all this, hmm? Prove your undying devotion.'

She frowned, unsure of what he wanted from her. 'Well, we would have to take it a day at a time, but we could try.'

'Well, let's take it a minute at a time now. Do as I ask and undress for me.'

She took a step back from him. 'You're serious, aren't you?' Her voice trembled slightly. She wanted his tenderness so much, but he kept bringing it back to this.

'Why—aren't *you*?'

He sounded so cold, so ruthless, and yet when he'd kissed her, when he'd touched her, she had imagined she'd glimpsed the man she had thought she loved once.

It was as if a veil was down between them now, and it didn't matter what she did, she kept getting tangled up in it. Maybe she always would. Maybe no matter what she did or said he would always think of her as the mercenary gold-digger who had deceived him.

And then, before she could analyse what she was doing, or why, she started to take off the white silk top.

Her blonde hair fell in disarray around her shoulders as she pulled the top over her head. She was wearing a plain white bra, not overtly sexy, just plain white cotton trimmed with satin. Yet its plainness made it the sexiest piece of underwear Damon had seen in a long time, due in no small way to the pert voluptuousness of her curves.

Her eyes held with his as she unfastened her skirt and let it fall to the floor.

His gaze travelled slowly down over her body, taking in

every detail. She was wearing a pair of white satin pants that curved prettily over her hips. Her figure was as toned and sensational as he'd remembered, her legs long and shapely.

'You still look as good as you did back then,' he told her gruffly. 'You always were an incredibly sexy woman.'

He watched the flare of colour in her skin. She looked embarrassed and shy, yet she stood straight and met his gaze with guileless, clear eyes. 'But I'm not the same,' she told him softly.

'No?' He felt his insides tighten and his need for her scream out as her hands went around to unfasten the bra.

'No. I've had a baby since then. It changed my body.'

The bra fell to the floor.

Her breasts were fantastic—large, yet so perfectly shaped and firm, her nipples still hard and erect from his touch.

'It changed you in a good way,' he told her softly. 'A very good way.'

Her hand played with the thin satin of her pants, and she cast him a look that shot molten heat through him. She looked so vulnerable, so nervous. He couldn't stand her looking at him like, that it ate him away.

'Come here.' Before she could take the underwear off, he reached and caught her arm and pulled her closer.

'I thought you wanted me to take all my clothes off?' The soft yet tremulous question tore at him. Was she close to tears? He felt like someone had struck him. He pulled her closer and into his arms, and allowed her to bury her head against his shoulder.

'No, it's OK.' His hand stroked down over the softness of her blonde hair and then the smooth, naked skin of her back. She felt good in his arms, too damned good. 'I know it's as you English like to say: collar and cuffs all match.'

He just held her for a moment, his mind racing. What the

hell was the matter with him? Why did he feel so bad? She was a teasing, tormenting witch! She deserved a bit of humiliation.

She turned her head slightly and cuddled in against him. His thumb brushed gently over the side of her face. Was it wet with tears?

'Abbie?'

The rasp of his voice aroused her so much. She turned her head, and suddenly they were kissing with a heat and a need that tore her apart. It was as if the spark had ignited, and everything around them had caught fire.

His hands caressed her naked body, finding her breasts, grazing over her nipples, his fingers teasing them, squeezing them until she gasped for pleasure. She found herself turned around, so that she was the one against the desk, and the next moment she was lying over it and she could feel the cold leather against her back.

His mouth moved to kiss her neck and then trail a blaze down to her breasts, finding her nipples, sucking on them, licking them.

She wound her arms around his neck. All she could think was that she wanted him urgently, wanted him now!

His hands stroked down over the satin material of her pants, stroking her through the material.

'Damon, have you got anything?'

'Hmm?' He lifted his head to look at her.

'Have you got any protection?'

He smiled. 'Yes…somewhere.' As he moved away from her slightly, the contracts on the desk slithered to the floor.

'Maybe that's an omen.' She looked up at him through the darkness of her lashes, her eyes sparkling and seductive. 'Maybe we don't need those contracts now.'

He stilled.

'I mean, we don't need to rush into getting married,' she

explained softly. She reached up to run her hands through the darkness of his hair. 'We can take our time, recapture the past, get to know each other again and—'

'Stop it, Abbie,' he cut across her roughly. 'We don't need to get to know each other again. And I certainly don't want to recapture the past. I know you well enough.'

The brutal words cut through the illusion of their tender love-making. Nothing had changed, she realised dully. She had been fooling herself to think that Damon could ever forget what she had done.

She watched as he zipped up his jeans, and then bent to pick up the contracts from the floor.

'You are not going to get round me—you will sign the contracts, Abbie. Otherwise there is no deal.'

His voice was perfectly controlled, and it was all a million miles away from the passion of just a few moments ago.

She shouldn't have mentioned the contracts. Why had she said anything? 'I wasn't trying to get round you,' she said softly.

'Of course not.' By contrast his voice was almost contemptuous, and her skin burned as his eyes flicked over her naked body.

'I did as you asked,' she reminded him, putting her arms over her breasts to shield them.

'And now you can do as I ask again.' He put the contracts down beside her and picked up a pen. 'Sign on the dotted line.'

Her breathing felt constricted. She had been so turned on…and his cold, merciless manner hurt so much.

'Fine!' She snapped the pen out of his hand and stood up from the desk. 'Show me where you want me to sign and let's just get it over with.'

'Very wise.' He turned the pages over for her and pointed to the last line. 'And don't forget to date it.'

He was unbelievable! Abbie's heart thumped fiercely against her chest as she scribbled her name and the date.

Damon watched her detachedly, and then he couldn't help but let his eyes wander over her figure.

She looked so good, her blonde hair swinging around her shoulders, brushing against her breasts. She still had on her high heels.

The erection that had been straining against his jeans earlier suddenly intensified.

'There.' She slammed the pen down and turned to look at him, her eyes filled with vehemence. 'Satisfied?'

'No, not yet.'

The tone of his voice had changed; his eyes were like liquid fire.

To her consternation, the look turned her on. She was furious with herself. Couldn't she just learn her lesson where he was concerned? She tried to move away from him but he caught her arm.

'Now we can consummate the deal,' he said softly.

She shook her head. 'Oh no, you don't get everything your own way, Damon.' To her horror her voice trembled with feeling. 'You want the *deal*—as you like to call it—done correctly. You marry me first.'

'You're such a spitfire when you want to be.' He paid no attention to her words, just pulled her closer. 'But at least now we've cut through all that rubbish about turning back the clock. If you think I'm going to forget what you really are, then you are mistaken.'

'Fine, have it your way.'

'Oh, don't worry—I will.' His eyes drifted down over her body, and to her dismay she found the way he looked at her made her breasts instantly harden and throb with need.

'I'll have it my way over and over again.' He smiled, but he let go of her. 'And I'll look forward to that tomorrow.'

She glared at him with a mixture of fury and regret. She

didn't want things to be like this between them. She didn't want to yearn for him…but she did.

Rather than bend to pick up her clothes, she left them on the floor and fled from the room. She would rather take her chances bumping into Elise than give Damon the pleasure of watching her gathering up her clothing wearing just her pants.

Luckily she made it to her bedroom without bumping into the housekeeper.

Mario was still fast asleep. The room was tranquil and silent, but there was no solace to be found for Abbie. In fact that very tranquility seemed to mock the tempestuous emotions swirling around inside her.

How could she have allowed herself to think for one moment that they could turn back time? Damon would never forget what she had done, and he would never, ever even consider the fact that he might be wrong about her.

He was so damned smug and superior! She kicked off her shoes and took off her pants, then went to stand under the cool, forceful jet of the shower.

Well, he could go to hell—she hated him!

But as her face turned upwards to the jet of water she remembered how he had so easily turned her on. And she knew that she didn't hate him at all. One moment she had been lost and desolate…the next he had stoked up a fierce longing inside her that had allowed her to return his kisses without reserve, had allowed her to speak without thinking.

She should never have mentioned those contracts. She was such an idiot. But she really had thought that maybe they could start to put things right. She kept remembering how good it could be between them.

Wrapping herself in a towel, she returned to the bedroom to get dressed. She found a black linen skirt in her bag, and a white T-shirt, and hurriedly put them on.

She needed to forget the way Damon made her feel and concentrate on reality, she told herself crossly. But as she reached to pick up a brush to tidy her hair the diamond ring on her finger flashed fire, reminding her that the reality for her was, from tomorrow onwards, she would be Damon's possession.

Mario woke up and started to cry. 'It's OK, honey. I'm coming.' Glad of the distraction, she put the brush down and hurried in to pick him up.

Mario was hungry, which meant going downstairs and facing Damon again. Her stomach tied into knots as she carried the child out into the hallway and down the stairs.

She peeped her head around the door of the study, but there was no sign of Damon. Her clothes, she noted, had been placed on a chair. Part of her wanted to go in and get them, then run back upstairs with them, but Mario was fidgeting in her arms. He needed something to eat, and he was starting to grizzle about the delay.

So, ignoring her discarded clothing, she carried on down the corridor in search of the kitchen. She found it without too much effort. It was at the back of the house, next door to a dining room that looked as if it was big enough to be used as a banqueting suite.

The kitchen was also massive. It had a black-and-white tiled floor and black counter-tops against pale-beech units. Elise was standing at the far end of the room, peeling and chopping vegetables, before throwing them into a pan on the black range cooker. She looked around with a smile. 'Ah, the little one is refreshed now?' Leaving her work, she came over to fuss over Mario. 'He is adorable, and he is so like his father!'

'Yes...' Abbie felt her heart contract at those words. 'But he's a bit crotchety because he's hungry.'

'Put him down.' Elise drew out a high chair from beside the kitchen table. 'I'll make him some lunch.'

Cots and now high chairs, Abbie noted dryly. *Damon has got himself organised.*

'Thank you, Elise, but I can manage. You continue with your work. I don't want to disturb you.' As Abbie put the child into the chair, she spotted the bag she had brought with her that contained all the paraphernalia Mario needed for meal times. Their driver must have brought it in—or maybe Damon. 'Have you seen Damon, by the way?'

She tried to sound nonchalant as she asked the question, but inside she felt taut with tension.

'He came in a few moments ago to tell me he's going over to his apartment in town to sort a few things out.' Elise glanced over at her with a smile. 'Congratulations on your engagement, by the way.'

'Thank you.' Abbie wondered if Elise found this situation as strange as she did. A whirlwind wedding and an unexpected child all catered for in the space of forty-eight hours—it was a lot for anyone to get his or her head around. And, in fairness to Damon, he must still be in shock himself from learning he was a father. 'Did Damon say when he'd be back?' She wanted to see him, to try and make things better again.

'I rather assumed he wouldn't be,' Elise answered with a frown. 'He said he would be sleeping there tonight as it might be bad luck to see his bride on the eve of the wedding.' She must have seen the look of surprise on Abbie's face because she immediately looked concerned. 'He didn't tell you?'

Abbie shook her head.

'Maybe you both have a touch of pre-wedding nerves, hmm?' Elise looked over at her with sudden sympathy.

She thinks we've had a lovers' tiff and Damon has marched

off, Abbie realised. She wished suddenly that it were that simple. 'Perhaps.' She shrugged evasively. She couldn't possibly begin to tell the woman what was really going on; it was far too embarrassing.

'Damon has been a bachelor who has enjoyed his freedom—this is a big step,' Elise said soothingly. 'He's bound to be a bit apprehensive...'

'Yes, I'm sure.' Abbie's tone was dry. She knew exactly what Elise meant when she said Damon was a bachelor who enjoyed his freedom—no doubt he'd enjoyed more women than there were days in the year. She'd seen the way women looked at him. He was like a magnet for them. As for feeling apprehensive now—she didn't think Damon was in the slightest bit worried. As far as he was concerned, he would be gaining a legalised mistress tomorrow, nothing more.

'And it is difficult for you too,' Elise was continuing smoothly. 'You have come to a new country, given up everything you know. It's exciting, but also scary. There is bound to be tension.'

'Yes.' Elise had definitely got the last bit of that statement right. 'I don't even know him that well,' she found herself admitting softly.

'Signor Cyrenci is a very honourable and decent man. He's had a lot of sadness, with the death of his father. Watching someone you love die...' Elise shook her head. 'Well, it was terrible for him. His father was such a good man, and so strong and vital until illness struck.'

'When was that?' Abbie asked softly.

'Must be over two years ago now.'

'Around the time he lost his business?' Abbie felt an ice-like chill start to seep through her.

Elise nodded. 'It was some time after that, yes.'

'I didn't know!' Abbie felt distraught. Had the stress of losing his business made Damon's father ill?

Elise shrugged. 'Well, it's in the past—Signor Cyrenci probably doesn't want to remember it. Things are happier now, and you are getting married tomorrow.' Elise smiled. 'I'm so pleased for you both. Signor Cyrenci deserves this chance of happiness.'

But the reassuring words didn't help at all; Abbie felt sick inside.

'Are you OK?' Elise was looking at her strangely now.

'Yes.' Abbie tried to pull herself together, but she wasn't OK—she was anything but OK.

No wonder Damon wanted to punish her. Maybe he blamed her for not only helping to ruin his father financially but also for contributing towards his death.

'Do you want to sit down? I'll look after Mario.'

The housekeeper's kindness made her want to cry. She didn't deserve any kindness. She was guilty. Guilty by association…guilty of having a father who wrecked lives. 'I don't want to put you to any trouble.'

'Nonsense, it is no trouble. I told Signor Cyrenci I will be glad to help with Mario. I have had three children of my own; two boys and a girl. They are all grown up now.'

Abbie was grateful for the cheerfully efficient tones soothing over her, and grateful when the woman took over from her to heat Mario's lunch. She really didn't feel capable of anything right now.

'Thank you, Elise.' She smiled tremulously at the woman. 'If you are sure, maybe I'll go into the garden for a few moments and get some fresh air.'

It was a relief to step outside the back door, a relief not to have to pretend that everything was all right. It sounded as if Damon's father had died as a result of her father's actions. She walked around the side of the house, the gravel crunching beneath her feet whilst her mind crunched over and over the past.

There was sweet warmth to the summer morning, but Abbie felt cold inside. Her father had ruined so many lives.

She remembered the emotions that had swamped her as she'd watched her mother's life ebbing away. The helplessness of the situation, merged with the anger—then the guilt. If she hadn't helped her mother to escape from her marriage, she would have got treatment sooner and then maybe she could have got better.

Did Damon feel like that when he looked at her? Did he think if he hadn't gone away with her to Palm Springs that his father might be alive today?

If so then he would never forgive her, because he could never forgive himself. Those kinds of feelings could eat you away inside.

She paused as she reached the front of the house and saw the silver-blue sports car that Damon had given her the keys to that morning. She didn't want his gifts. She didn't want his money. All she wanted was to make things better between them again. But that hope seemed further away than ever now.

'Come out to admire your new acquisition, I see.'

Damon's mocking tones made her whirl around in surprise. He was standing a few yards away from her on the front doorstep, watching her. She noticed he'd changed into a pair of black jeans teamed with a black T-shirt. He looked heart-wrenchingly handsome, every inch the haughty Sicilian, master of all he surveyed.

Tomorrow he would be her husband. The knowledge drummed inside her with insistent force.

And then what would happen between them?

'Actually, I was just getting some fresh air.' She hastily tried to pull herself together. 'Elise told me you'd gone to your apartment in town.'

'I have one or two loose ends to tie up here first.'

She nodded and looked away from him. 'At least you've got the business side of things taken care of for our wedding tomorrow.' She tried to sound nonchalant.

Damon watched her through narrowed eyes. There was something poignant about the way she said that. She looked so innocent, so...

He swore under his breath. What the hell was the matter with him? She looked sad because he'd forced her to sign his contract, and she knew now that she wouldn't be able to have a quickie divorce in a few months' time and walk away with his fortune.

That was the type of person she was, and he couldn't allow her big blue eyes and gorgeous figure to cloud that reality in his mind.

He couldn't believe that in the office this morning he'd been filled with remorse for what he was doing to her—filled with shame for making her undress. And all the time she had been the one trying to seduce him into throwing away the prenuptial contract!

And now here she was, out surveying her car—weighing up how much it was worth, no doubt.

She was treacherous!

'Yes, the business side of things is in place,' he replied coolly. 'All we need now is the piece of paper from the registrar.'

She nodded and moved to push her blonde hair out of her face as a soft breeze caught it. The silky tumble of her hair around her shoulders made him think about how she had looked when she'd pulled her top off this morning.

He'd wanted her so much. He'd never desired any woman as much as her. How he had managed to regain his control and pull back from her, he didn't know. All he did know was that tomorrow he would make up for lost time; he would take her again and again until he'd purged some of this need for her out of his body.

'So it's to be a civil ceremony?' She maintained eye contact with him, and tried not to flinch from the fire in his eyes as he watched her.

'Of course it is. Were you hoping for a big high-society wedding? A white dress, your father giving you away perhaps?'

The derisive tone hurt. 'I wasn't hoping for anything.' She tried to angle her chin up a little further. 'I tried to tell you that this morning, that we could just live together...' She struggled for the right words, but she couldn't find them.

As she looked up into his eyes she wanted to tell him that she was sorry about his father—that she was desperately sorry for the part she had played, that she would try to make things up to him...in any way he wanted. But she couldn't say any of it; the words were stuck amidst a well of tears lodged deep inside.

Damon shook his head and came closer to her. 'No, darling Abbie, I think it's best that our arrangement is written down in black and white. You will marry me tomorrow and become a dutiful wife and mother.'

The scorn was sizzling, but she didn't rise to it. 'I'll do whatever you want, Damon,' she said softly instead.

Damon felt a flare of exhilaration as he realised he'd finally brought her to heel.

CHAPTER SEVEN

IT WAS her wedding day.

As Abbie stood in her bedroom and surveyed her reflection in the cheval mirror, she still couldn't quite believe that it was happening—that she was going to marry Damon Cyrenci.

As a little girl she had always maintained quite staunchly that when she grew up she would never get married. She supposed her parents' marriage had put her off; John and Elizabeth Newland had certainly not been a glowing advertisement for the institution.

She remembered telling her mother once when she'd been about ten that she didn't even want a boyfriend let alone a husband. Her mother had laughed. 'Abbie, when you grow up and find someone you truly love then you will change your mind. And I hope when you do that you find the kind of man who is protective and tender and strong—someone who lets you find your wings and soar. With that kind of love, you can conquer the world.'

Why was she thinking about that now? Abbie blinked back the tears. She couldn't think about her mother today—this was already hard enough.

Her eyes drifted down over her suit. She was wearing an ivory silk pencil-skirt that finished just under the knee, teamed with a matching nipped-in jacket that showed off her tiny waist and the swell of her breast.

On Damon's insistence she had allowed his chauffeur to drop her into town yesterday afternoon so that she could buy something to wear.

'Buy some new lingerie as well,' Damon had instructed as he'd peeled some notes out of his wallet.

She'd turned away from him before he'd been able to press the money into her hand. 'I can afford my own dress and underwear, Damon,' she had told him forcefully.

'But we both know that what you really want is to spend this…don't we?' He'd pulled her back and tucked the notes down into her bra.

Just thinking about that now made her upset and furious all over again.

He really thought that she was just interested in money. She bit down on her lip. She understood why he thought that. From his point of view she had lived off her father's ill-gotten profits without shame or remorse. She was calculating and mercenary. There was nothing she could say that would change the past. She had done what she had done and Damon's father had died a broken man. She could only hope that once they were married he would get to know the real her, would realise she had never meant to hurt him, and that deep down she wasn't a bad person.

Damon hadn't been there when she'd returned from her shopping trip. He'd spent the night at his apartment in town. Elise had told her that he would meet her today at the town hall, where they would be married.

She wondered how he had spent his last night as a bachelor, and how he was feeling this morning. What was he thinking? Had he spent the night with another woman?

That thought brought a punch with it that really hurt.

There was a knock on the door. 'The car is ready and waiting whenever you are,' Elise called out cheerfully.

But would Damon be ready and waiting for her? Maybe he'd decided that a marriage without love wasn't worth having, and maybe he was right except the thought of him walking away from her now hurt so much she could hardly breathe.

'Abbie?' Elise knocked on the door again. 'You're running a little late.'

With difficulty Abbie pulled herself together and went to open the door.

'Oh, you look so beautiful.' Elise smiled with delight as she saw her.

'Thank you.' Abbie reached to take her son from the woman. 'Has he been good for you?'

'A little angel,' Elise said quickly. 'Now, you mustn't worry about him this afternoon. I'll take good care of him.'

Abbie nodded. She'd wanted to bring Mario with her to the ceremony, but Damon had insisted that he stay behind with Elise.

'A few minutes and it will all be over,' he'd told her firmly. 'Why disrupt his routine? He has an afternoon nap, is that not so?'

'Yes, but—'

'Then we will leave him to his sleep. He is a baby, Abbie. He won't know what is going on. What happens between us tomorrow is between consenting adults. The only thing that will be important to Mario is that he has both his parents with him as he grows up.'

Abbie hugged the child close now, and he wriggled in her arms. He was tired; she could see his eyes starting to close.

'I'll put him down in a few minutes,' Elise told her soothingly. 'Then I'll turn on the baby monitor and listen out for him.'

'Come up and check on him as well,' Abbie said. 'Just in case…'

'Yes. Please don't worry. I know all about taking care of babies. I'm not just a mother, I'm also a grandmother.'

With a smile Abbie handed her baby back over to the woman. She knew Mario would be fine with Elise. She was capable and kind, and Mario seemed to like her. Her real worry was what lay ahead of her.

Elise accompanied her back down the stairs, and stood framed in the doorway with Mario in her arms as she watched Abbie getting into the limousine.

The white-hot heat of the afternoon made the atmosphere strangely silent, as if everything was lulled into sleep. The scent of lavender and jasmine was heavy in the air. The chauffeur closed the door and climbed behind the wheel. Abbie waved at Elise and Mario, then settled back into the empty silence of the car.

She watched the scenery pass by. For a while there was an arid landscape of cacti, then dazzling mountain villages surrounded by lemon-and-orange groves against the backdrop of a cerulean blue sky.

The limousine pulled into a village square and ground to a halt under the shade of a large tree. Abbie thought that they would be getting married in the city where she had shopped for her outfit yesterday, but this town was quaintly charming, and had almost a surreal, romantic feel about it.

She smiled sadly at the thought. She was sure Damon hadn't chosen this location for any reasons of the heart.

She looked around. The buildings were painted a dazzling white and the narrow streets were cobbled. Somewhere a bell was chiming. But there wasn't a soul about. Abbie wondered where Damon was. Maybe he had stood her up. Maybe she'd been right about last night.

A black cat asleep under the shade of the tree uncurled to watch with curious green eyes as the chauffeur opened the car door for her.

Then as she stepped into the heat of the afternoon she looked up, and her glance met with Damon's.

Abbie felt her heart dart with a burst of pure pleasure.

He was standing at the top of some steps leading into an impressive-looking building. He looked so handsome in the formal suit, his dark hair glinting in the sun, that she found herself rooted to the spot just drinking him in, committing this moment to memory.

The car door slammed closed behind her, bringing her back to reality, and she walked slowly across to where he was waiting.

Although he was leaning nonchalantly against the pillar of the doorway, there was nothing casual about the way he was watching her. She noticed his dark Sicilian eyes held that blatantly bold look—a look that took in everything about her from her high heels to the way she had secured her hair up. A look that practically undressed her and made her sizzle inside with tension, but also with an answering need, a need that she didn't even want to try and acknowledge right at this moment.

'Hello.' As she reached his side, she smiled up at him uncertainly. What did one say in this situation? 'Am I late?' She cringed—that sounded absurd given the circumstances.

But he smiled back, his lips tugging in a crooked line. 'As a matter of fact, you are. But you were worth the wait.'

The husky undertone made her warm inside. 'That's all right, then.' She tried to sound nonchalant.

'I suppose it is.' He held out a hand. 'So, shall we go get this over with?'

She hesitated for just a moment before putting her hand in his and allowing him to lead her inside.

The possessive touch of his skin against hers made her even more nervous. It was dark inside the building, dark and cool. Her high heels echoed on the marble floors as he led her towards another door and opened it.

The room they walked into had a high ceiling and an ornate upper gallery. A large stained-glass window filtered sunshine in shafts of red and blue across the large wooden table at the top. Behind it there was a throne-like chair and a stand that held both the Sicilian and the Italian flags.

Wooden seating was arranged in the auditorium, probably enough for fifty people. But only a group of three waited for them at the top of the room, a woman and two men. All were dressed smartly. The men wore grey suits and the woman, who was an attractive brunette of perhaps forty, was wearing a blue business-like trouser suit.

'Signor Cyrenci.' The woman reached to shake his hand, and Damon let go of Abbie to greet her. For a moment the conversation was in rapid Italian and then the woman smiled at Abbie. 'My apologies, Ms Newland, I didn't realise you didn't speak Italian. The ceremony today will be conducted in English. We have two witnesses for you, Luigi Messini and Alfredi Grissillini, both clerks who work here.' The woman smoothly introduced the men to her, and they nodded their heads in acknowledgement. 'Now, shall we proceed?'

As Abbie and Damon moved to take two chairs placed before the table, the woman took the throne-like seat behind.

This all felt unreal, Abbie thought as she listened to the woman talking about the institution of marriage whilst at the same time taking out some documentation from a drawer.

She glanced over at Damon, who was listening intently. Her eyes moved over his rugged features, taking in the firm, square jaw, the sensual curve of his lips, the aristocratic nose. His thick hair gleamed an almost blue-black streaked with just a few strands of silver at the temple; it was brushed back from his face in an almost careless manner. She loved his hair, loved running her fingers through it when he kissed her.

The thought of him kissing her made her stomach do a weird flip of desire.

She glanced away from him hurriedly as the woman asked them both to stand.

'Abigail Newland, do you take this man, Damon Allessio Cyrenci, as your lawfully wedded husband? Do you promise to love, honour and obey him and for all time stay true only to him?'

Abbie looked over at Damon. He was watching her with an unfathomable expression in his dark eyes. She felt her heart speed up, hitting against her ribcage with a fierce intensity that was almost painful.

'I do.'

He smiled, and she tried to pull her thoughts together as they jumbled together inside her in the craziest of emotions.

'Damon Allessio Cyrenci, do you take this woman, Abigail, as your lawfully wedded wife, to have and to hold from this day forward?'

It wasn't lost on Abbie that the vows he took were different from hers. He'd written what he wanted. He'd made her promise to obey him—whilst he'd promised only to have and to hold. Damon did what he wanted, and was asserting that this was the way it would be from now on.

She felt a surge of pure anger. But as he took her hand in his, and slipped the plain gold band into place, he smiled at her and this time there was something in his eyes that stilled her anger.

'I now pronounce you man and wife.' The woman smiled at them. 'May I be the first to congratulate you on your new life together.'

'Thank you.' Damon didn't break eye contact with Abbie as he answered, and for a moment it was almost as if he were saying thank you to her.

'I suppose we should seal the deal with a kiss…hmm?' he asked her softly. He didn't wait for a reply. He leaned down, and his lips grazed tenderly over hers.

The sensual feeling sent shivers of desire racing through her entire body. She kissed him back tentatively, yet she desperately wanted more, wanted this place and these strangers to melt away and leave them alone to finish what they had started such a long time ago.

Damon pulled back from her, and then it was time for them to sign the register.

Abbie watched the coloured shafts of light slant over the papers, the light turning them to rose pink then to gold as they were moved for her signature. A few minutes later they were outside again in the fierce sun.

Had that really happened? Was she really married? Abbie looked up at the handsome Sicilian beside her. He was a stranger to her in so many ways, and yet so achingly familiar.

Damon glanced down at her and smiled. 'So, how are you feeling, Mrs Cyrenci?'

Abbie didn't know how she was feeling. 'Shell-shocked, I think,' she admitted softly.

Their chauffeur opened the doors of the limousine for them, and it was a relief to slip into the air-conditioned cool.

A bottle of champagne waited for them on ice, and Damon sat opposite her to uncork it as the vehicle glided smoothly out of the square.

He handed a glass across to her, and then sat back to give her his undivided attention.

How was it that he only had to look at her like that and the adrenalin started pumping wildly through her body? Was it something about his eyes? He did have the sexiest eyes of any man she'd ever met. Or was it his aura? He did radiate a powerful magnetism. Whatever it was, it really got to Abbie, made her temperature soar so much that she wanted to melt, made her heart race, made her body tingle with pleasure, made her think about the pleasure he could give her…

Hurriedly she looked away from him. Silence stretched between them. She felt awkward. She felt like she needed to say something to break the tension rising inside her.

'I can't believe that we actually got married,' she managed at last.

His lips curved in a smile. 'Well, we did. And you made a very sexy bride. I like the outfit.'

'Thank you.'

'Your hair also looks good like that.'

His eyes moved over her face, noticing the velvety softness of her skin, the blush of her cheeks and the peach-satin sheen of her lips.

She'd taken his breath away when she'd stepped out of the car. He'd never wanted anyone as much as he'd wanted her at that moment. The suit was perfect: sexy yet sophisticated. And her hair was also perfect—also sophisticated, but the tendrils that had escaped to curl around the beauty of her face gave her softness and a fragile vulnerability that tore him up inside.

She raised her blue eyes towards him now and he felt the same wrenching feeling inside. He wished he could rid himself of this sensation. He wanted to feel lust for her, nothing more…

'I told Frederic to drive us back to my apartment in town. The staff there will have laid us out a late lunch. And then I'm taking you to bed for the afternoon.' He said the words in a low, commanding tone and watched as her skin flared with colour. 'Are you hungry?'

Abbie hurriedly glanced away from him. Her heart was racing. She didn't want to eat. She didn't know what she wanted…

The thought of spending the afternoon in bed with Damon was infinitely exciting, yet terrifying, all at the same time.

'Not really.' She didn't dare look over at him. She felt foolish and unsure of everything. 'And don't you think we should go back to the house, not to your apartment? I want to check on Mario.'

'Mario will still be asleep.' Damon reached across and topped up her glass of champagne. 'And Elise is very trust-worthy.'

She couldn't argue with that.

Would he ask her to undress the way he had yesterday… Would he be gentle? In the past Damon had always been a passionate yet sensitive lover. She remembered the tenderness in his kiss yesterday, and a floodgate of feelings for him opened up that truly terrified her.

She took a few hurried sips of her champagne and then put the glass down in the holder next to her.

Damon watched as she nervously fiddled with a couple of buttons on her jacket.

'You should take that off now,' he instructed.

Something about the instruction made her nerves stretch even more. 'Damon, I know you got me to promise that I would obey you, but I have to inform you right now that it is not a promise I intend to keep.' She suddenly angled her chin up and sent him a look of fierce defiance from her flashing eyes.

To her disconcertment he merely looked amused at her outburst. 'Breaking your vows already?' He mocked her with dark eyes. 'Dear me, Abbie…' He shook his head. 'That simply just won't do.'

'No, it won't!' She lowered her tone but her voice trembled alarmingly. 'I may be your wife, but I have my own mind, Damon. There are certain things that I will not be told about.'

'And what are they?' Damon sounded like he was enjoying himself—as if she were the most entertaining of women.

'What to wear, what to do—and on the subject of Mario—'

'On the subject of Mario we will confer and decide things together,' he cut across her firmly and smiled. 'You are his mother, and I respect that.'

The words took her aback, took the fire out of her argument.

'But as for what you wear and what you do especially in the bedroom…on that you will defer to me.'

His arrogance inflamed her senses, yet the melting eyes that held with hers made the warm darts of desire increase inside her.

She looked away from him, annoyed with herself.

'And by the way when I told you to take your jacket off it was because I thought you looked uncomfortable,' he added. 'I wasn't going to tell you to take everything else off as well.' He glanced at her. 'Well, not yet, anyway.'

'Very amusing.' Abbie fought down the flood of heat inside her. He thought he was so clever. 'And I can't believe you made me promise to obey you.' She shook her head.

Damon laughed. 'Well, you were late. I thought I'd fill the time waiting for you in a productive manner.'

The limousine pulled up by a marina. Luxury yachts bobbed on tranquil clear water, and there were some upmarket boutiques and restaurants. The place had a very sophisticated feel. It was obviously a playground for the moneyed, yet it still retained a charm and character from the past. Fisherman sat mending their nets by the harbour wall, and the new buildings along the quay merged seamlessly with old.

'My apartment is just here.' Damon pointed to a modern building.

It was all very swish, Abbie thought as she followed him into the foyer. A security guard greeted him by name, and then they stepped into a lift.

Damon's apartment was at the top of the building. By contrast with his house, it was ultra-modern to the point of minimalist. A bachelor's playground, Abbie thought as she glanced around, all tubular steel and appliances of science. Wall-mounted TV's, remote-control gadgets for everything, probably even the cooker. And the bed... Her eyes skimmed past the room that held the enormous king-sized bed.

Damon opened doors that led out to a large terrace. They were high up, and the view was spectacular across the harbour and the alluring blue glitter of the sea.

Someone had gone to a lot of trouble, and had set a table outside for lunch. The table was covered with a crisp white-linen cloth, and was laid with silver and crystal ware. An ice bucket held a bottle of champagne, and there were balloons everywhere across the wooden decking.

Damon shook his head as he surveyed the scene. 'I made the mistake of telling the staff that it was my wedding day—they must have thought balloons were a nice touch.'

'They are.' The fact that someone had gone to that trouble somehow touched Abbie. She met Damon's steady gaze and shrugged. 'Well, I like them...it's lovely.'

His lips twisted in an amused smile. 'There's something you'll probably like a little better waiting for you on the table.'

She saw the jewellery box sitting on the white place-setting, but didn't go to pick it up. 'What is it?' she asked him huskily.

'A little bauble to mark our wedding day. Go and have a look.'

Before she could answer, the ring of Damon's mobile phone interrupted them. He glanced at the dial before answering, then disappeared inside for a few moments.

Abbie could hear him talking in Italian, but she was barely listening. Why couldn't he get it through his head that she didn't want his gifts? She opened the box and glanced inside. Nestling on velvet was an exquisite necklace, a single diamond teardrop on a gold chain. It was probably worth a fortune.

For a moment her mind ran back to their conversation when he'd first suggested they get married, and she had rounded on him in outrage. *'You think I'd tie myself into a loveless marriage…?'*

'For wealth, security and all the baubles and trappings of luxury you could possibly want? Yes I do.'

She snapped the lid closed and put the box down as if it had burnt her. Then she moved towards the balustrade to look down at the harbour, but tears blinded her eyes.

'So, do you like the necklace?' Damon appeared behind her again.

She didn't answer him, couldn't answer him.

'It is real,' he told her dryly.

She closed her eyes. She understood why he thought of her the way he did—she just wished it didn't hurt.

His phone rang again, and after a moment's hesitation he took the call. 'Sorry about that,' he murmured a moment later. 'I've got an important deal going through soon.'

Abbie had been glad of the interruption; at least it had given her a moment to pull herself together. 'That's all right, you've got to get your priorities in order.'

'Well, today *you* are my priority—so I've switched the phone off now.'

She wished he meant that. She stared pensively out across the expanse of sea.

'So, shall we have something to eat?'

'I told you, I'm not really hungry.' She felt too tense to eat, too tense to even look around at him. 'I don't know what we are doing here. We should really have just gone back to the house.'

'You know what we are doing here, Abbie,' he told her softly.

She closed her eyes. 'Mario will be waking up soon.'

'Mario will be fast asleep.'

Abbie didn't say anything. She knew he was right, she knew she had no need to worry about Mario. She just wished that Damon hadn't bought her that necklace; she just wished that things between them were different. That the silly balloons meant something to him! What on earth was the matter with her? How stupid was that? she mocked herself fiercely.

She pulled herself together and blinked the tears away. Then, steeling herself, she turned to look at him.

'Elise told me about your father,' she said suddenly.

'What did she tell you?' he asked coolly.

'About his death—you know, soon after him losing the business, and…I just wanted to tell you how sorry I am. And I never wanted any of that to happen.'

The sincerity in her voice and in her eyes perplexed him.

'Well, I suggest we forget about the past and about the outside world for now, and relax.'

'But you can't forget about the past, can you?' she asked softly. 'And your father died because of it!'

'My father died because he smoked heavily all of his life,' Damon said with a frown.

'Oh! I thought… I thought it was the stress of losing the business.'

Damon watched the emotions flicker through her eyes. She looked like she had been genuinely distressed by the notion— but he only had to remember how cold-blooded she had been in the past to know that it was another of her little acting ploys. A woman who cared about hurting people didn't go around deceiving them, lying to them, didn't deliberately use her body to hurt others and get what she wanted.

'Abbie, you didn't contribute to his death, but you are right about one thing—I can't forget about the past or what you are. Because I'd be a fool to forget it.' His eyes swept over her suddenly and the contempt in them lashed at her.

'Feeling like that, I'm surprised you went through with the wedding,' she whispered rawly.

'On the contrary, when you stepped out of the car today and into the square I knew positively that I was doing the right thing.'

'Did you?' Her eyes lifted to his. 'Why?'

He looked at her for a long, considered moment and she could feel her heart racing against her chest.

'Because we have a child to look after. Mario has to come first now.'

Given the circumstances she knew she should be content with that, but the coldness of his response added to the ache inside her.

She watched as he turned away from her and lifted the bottle of champagne.

'Let's have a drink.'

He was so cavalier and nonchalant, and it made Abbie's temper rise. 'It's very noble of you, putting your needs to one side for your child's security,' she grated sardonically.

'Who said anything about putting my needs to one side?' He flashed her an amused look and she felt herself blush. 'I have absolutely no intention of doing that.'

He passed her the glass of champagne, and she was annoyed to find that her hand wasn't quite steady as she accepted it.

'But I want things to be right for Mario,' he continued smoothly. 'I know what it's like to grow up without a parent, Abbie. My mother walked out when I was eight, and… Well, I always vowed that I'd never put a child through that. A child needs stability. Bringing up a family is the ultimate commitment.'

'Is that why you decided to just play the field for all these years?'

He looked over at her wryly. 'Being a bachelor was something I was good at,' he said, his mouth curved with amusement.

Abbie remembered her suspicions earlier that morning, that Damon had been out last night enjoying himself, had brought someone back here to bed.

'And, now that we are married, do you *still* intend to play around?' She forced herself to ask the question even though she wasn't sure she wanted to hear the answer.

Damon watched the way her chin slanted up. What was she thinking? he wondered. Despite the valiant angle of her chin, there was a husky tone to her voice, and that look in her eyes…

He frowned and dragged his thoughts away from the absurd wayward direction they wanted to go in. Abbie's greatest concern was probably only the fact that, if he found someone else, she might lose her golden ticket to riches.

'I thought I made my intentions clear—I want a stable home for Mario.' He held her gaze steadily. 'So I intend to amuse myself playing around with *you* from now on.'

She flushed a little and he smiled. 'I think you will manage to keep me satisfied. You are very attractive, very beautiful, Abbie—but then of course you know that don't you.'

The compliment sat painfully with her.

Damon watched the shadowy, dark glints of sapphire in her eyes. She was so desirable, he felt his stomach tie up with the thought of having her now…felt himself harden. He just wished she didn't stir up these other emotions inside him.

Like now, for example; something in her expression made him long to forget what she was and reach out to hold her tenderly. It had been the same today when she'd stepped out of the car into the square, and also when she'd looked up at him whilst taking her vows.

She wasn't going to get under his skin ever again, Damon reminded himself fiercely. When he touched her, when he held her, it would be to take her, possess her, use her the way she had once used him.

He picked up his own glass of champagne. 'So what shall we drink to—the future, hmm? Our new arrangement?'

'How about your new acquisition?' she supplied, her eyes sparkling with that mixture of defiance and rawness that he was starting to know so well.

'Or to Mario?' he suggested. 'The one thing we got absolutely right?'

She smiled at him suddenly, and it was like the sun had come out from behind the clouds.

His eyes moved over her slowly. 'So, here we are, Mrs Cyrenci...alone at last.' His voice was teasingly sexy.

'Are we?' She tried not to sound apprehensive. 'Where are the staff?'

'All gone. We have a very good arrangement that gives me maximum privacy.'

'Everyone around you is very cooperative.'

'Apart from one...' His eyes moved down over her body with a possessiveness that made her pulses race. 'My wife. The woman who has already informed me today that she intends to break her wedding vows.'

She tried not be affected by the way he was looking at her, but she was. And his teasing tone brought her skin out in strange little goosebumps. She liked the way he referred to her as his wife in that warm way, as if it did mean something to him.

But it doesn't, she tried to remind herself fiercely. He'd already made that clear. She didn't mean anything to him.

Even so when he reached out and trailed one finger along

the side of her face she felt herself melt inside. 'You belong to me now, Abbie,' he said huskily. 'And that means keeping the promises you made today.'

Her heart hammered fiercely against her chest as she looked up at him. 'I'll keep the ones that are most important,' she whispered.

Something about the way she said that, the way she looked at him seared him to the bone. He watched as she put down her glass, reached to unfasten the buttons on her jacket and then slipped it off.

Underneath she wore a peach satin camisole with spaghetti straps. It emphasised the firm upward tilt of her breasts.

Abbie looked up at him and saw the flare of desire in the darkness of his eyes. She liked the way he looked at her. But she knew he didn't love her. She knew what he thought of her.

Still, he did want her. And she needed him to want her. Needed him to fill the aching void inside her. He was the one man she had never really got out of her system. She didn't understand why, and she didn't want to dwell too deeply on the questions. All she knew was how he could make her feel. And she wanted to feel like that again.

'How private are we out here?' She looked up at him from under dark eyelashes.

'About as private as you can get. Why don't you put on the gift I bought for you and take off everything else?'

The seductive comment inflamed her senses. 'I don't want your gift, Damon.' She continued to looked up at him through cloudy blue eyes.

He reached out a hand and stroked it softly down the side of her neck. The caress made her tingle inside. 'Well, I want your gift to me…and I want it right now.'

His fingers moved lower, teasingly stroking her along the edge of the camisole top.

The touch of his fingers brushing against her skin felt so good. She knew what he was talking about, and she didn't try to misunderstand him. There was no point in pretending, not when the gravelly command had made her body burn with a need to comply.

'So…what do you want to do?'

Damon liked the question—liked the way she matched it with a shy, almost faltering look in her big eyes.

'Should I do this…?' He watched as she unfastened her skirt and let it drop to the floor. She was wearing hold-up stockings, and she looked so sexy that he felt he wanted to burst with the intensity of his need for her.

'You should definitely do that,' he told her quietly.

'And how far do you want to go?'

'You know how far I want to go, Abbie,' he instructed. 'All the way.'

CHAPTER EIGHT

HER top followed her skirt onto the floor.

His eyes moved over her body. Her underwear, unlike yesterday, was deliberately provocative. The bra pushed her up, showing the round peaks of her breasts to perfection, her lace pants were hipsters but see-through and as for the lace-top stockings... Well, they were just too sexy for words.

Hell, he wanted her, wanted to fill her completely...possess her completely.

The way he was looking at her made Abbie feel taut with need. She wanted him to take her into his arms, wanted desperately just to be held. 'So...shall I help you out of your jacket?' It was an excuse for her to move closer to him. 'Perhaps unfasten your tie for you?' Her hands slid up over his chest to smooth the jacket away from the breadth of his shoulders. It fell to the floor with her clothes.

She looked up into his eyes as she reached to unfasten his tie.

Before he could think about how or where he wanted her, he was picking her up and turning her so that her back was against the wall. 'You know exactly what you do to me, don't you, with those big blue oh-so-innocent eyes...?'

Her eyes locked with his as she looked up at him breathlessly, and then she trembled as he slowly and deliberately ran his hands over her body, stroking over the curves of her breasts, his fingers finding her nipples through the lace of her bra and squeezing them. The caress shot exquisite darts of pleasure through her body, and like shots of an addictive drug the feelings made her long for so much more.

He smiled as he heard her gasp with need. Then his mouth moved to possess her lips. The kiss was like nothing she had ever experienced before, masterful, fierce; it sent a feeling of passion so strong, so fierce, racing through her that she felt dizzy…possessed, almost. She opened her mouth and let him plunder the softness inside. All the time she could feel the hard warmth of his body pressing against the aching need of hers.

Just when she thought she was going to die with the desire to be closer, to be possessed totally, he pulled back.

'Don't stop!' Her eyes were wild with tumultuous feelings of desire. 'Please, Damon…' She didn't have to go on because suddenly she felt his fingers stroking her through her knickers.

She was wet and ready for him, and as he stroked her some more she shuddered.

'You like that, don't you?' He whispered the words against her ear.

She closed her eyes. Her breasts felt so tight, so hard; they were throbbing with the demand to be touched. Her body was telling her that she had to have him…it was telling her with such insistent force that she couldn't think straight.

Then suddenly she felt him pushing her knickers down and moving her legs further apart, touching her in a way that took her breath away.

She moaned with pleasure when at the same time he pulled her bra down and bent his head to suck on her nipples.

Her body convulsed with enjoyment, and she raked her

fingers through the darkness of his hair, giving herself up to him with a total lack of control.

Just as she thought she was going to die of sheer pleasure, he left her.

'Damon?' The momentary uncertainty in her eyes was almost his undoing.

'We'll continue this inside.'

He took hold of her hand to lead her through to the bedroom.

It was taking every inch of his willpower not to lose control. He wanted her. Just watching her in those high heels, the stockings lovingly curving around her slender thighs... He needed to contain himself, he reminded himself fiercely. But as she sat down on the bed he could hardly wait to get rid of his clothes.

She noticed that he tore his shirt whilst unbuttoning it... She'd made him do that. The knowledge gave her a flip of exhilaration, but it was nothing to the way she felt as her eyes moved over the sheer perfection of his physique.

His body was toned and strong, tapering down to the perfect six-pack. Abbie remembered his body very well, remembered having been in awe of him when she had first seen him naked. Those feelings hadn't changed.

He joined her down on the bed and she made to take off her stockings, but he lifted her up and moved her back against the satin pillows. 'Stay as you are.' He growled the words against her skin as his mouth moved to capture hers again.

His kiss was ragged with need, his fingers insistent as once more they found her nipples, rubbing over them, pushing her bra down further so that they were forced upwards for his mouth to take possession of them again.

He straddled her, and then reached for some contraception before his body captured hers with fervent, demanding thrusts.

She writhed and gasped with pleasure, and then he pulled back from her a little, stroking her tenderly, finding her lips and kissing her with such sweetness, his hands stroking her hair.

He murmured her name almost incoherently as his body dominated hers, taking her with almost ruthless determination and yet at the same time with an exquisite care, possessing her with ardent warmth that made answering warmth flood her body.

He looked down into her eyes and murmured something to her in Italian.

'I like the sound of your voice when you speak in your own language,' she murmured breathlessly. She moaned and arched her back, and ran her fingers down over the powerful muscles of his back.

He said something else that she didn't understand…then took her lips with his, before grazing down her neck to her nipples to suck on them, lick them, and rock her towards a climax that was so forceful and shattering in its intensity that she cried out. Only then did he join her, releasing himself as wave after wave of sheer joy racked through both of their bodies, fusing them together as one.

For a long time they just lay there holding each other. Abbie felt like crying, not with sadness but with sheer joy, because making love with him had been as incredible as she'd remembered. Once again he had conjured up all the crazy feelings of belonging, and had strangely given the power of his love-making a sense of such sweet tenderness.

But this wasn't love, it was just sex, she tried to remind herself fiercely before she got too carried away on flights of fantasy. But the trouble was it didn't feel like it was just sex. She frowned and cuddled a bit closer to him. When he held her, especially like this, the feeling was blissful. It was like the real thing…like she never needed to be lonely again because he was her soul mate.

She closed her eyes and tried to stop analyzing things. It was enough to be in his arms.

He stroked his fingers through her hair almost absentmindedly, and then kissed the top of her head.

It was such a tender gesture that she let her breath out in a sigh. 'Making love with you is so…so good.'

'Yes, the chemistry is as powerful as ever between us. I knew it would be.'

She rolled over a little so that she was looking down at him. 'It is powerful, isn't it?' she breathed huskily. 'You turn me on so much.'

'I noticed.' He smiled at her suddenly, his eyes teasing.

'I kind of noticed that I had a similar effect on you.' She snuggled against him. 'Apart from the obvious—I think you ruined a perfectly good shirt.'

He laughed. 'So how are you with a darning needle, Mrs Cyrenci?'

She smiled. The connection between them felt so strong, the outside world had ceased to exist. Surely he couldn't have made love to her with such searing passion if he felt nothing for her? She wondered, if she took the risk of telling him a little of how she felt right now, would he meet her half way? 'No one's ever made me feel the way you make me feel,' she admitted.

Their eyes locked together, and for a heart-stopping moment she thought he was going to say something similar back to her. She felt so close to him, not just physically but emotionally.

Damon hesitated. She sounded as if she'd really meant that, and there was no doubt that her responses to him had been wildly passionate—she really had wanted him. Making love with her always had been incredible, and it had been better now than he'd even remembered. He felt like he couldn't get enough of holding her, teasing her to arousal, caressing her, kissing her… He frowned. But of course this wasn't making love—there was no emotion involved, he reminded himself fiercely. He had to remember exactly what Abbie was.

Yes, she enjoyed sex, but even the most mercenary of creatures did. Probably what aroused Abbie so much was the thought of all his money.

He ran a tender hand down over the side of her face. That knowledge was difficult to accept when she was looking at him with such sultry blue eyes. But he had to accept it. And at least she did enjoy sex with him—because if she didn't, well, he'd never forced a woman in his life and he certainly wasn't going to start now. 'And that's why our arrangement is going to work so well.' He growled the words against her ear.

Pain spiralled inside her from nowhere. She hadn't expected a declaration of undying love—but she hadn't thought he would remind her quite so dismissively that this was just an arrangement. She could be so stupid sometimes where he was concerned. She pulled away from him abruptly.

'Yes, I suppose you are right.' She tried to match his flippancy so that she could hang on to at least a small shred of pride. She should have known better than to risk lowering any barriers.

Damon watched as she moved away from him, and he was aware of a sudden sharp feeling of regret, as if a precious moment had been lost.

What the hell was the matter with him? He was supposed to be using her for his own pleasure—not making passionate declarations! But for one wild moment he wanted to pull her back, wanted to tell her that she had the same effect on him. That no other woman could make him feel the way she could.

He was losing it, Damon told himself furiously. It had been the same when they were making love: one moment he had been totally enjoying himself with her, and the next she had sighed and cuddled into him and the feelings inside him had completely changed with a swiftness and a power that he'd had no control over. He'd wanted her so much…wanted to hold her close and pleasure her.

He watched as she sat up from him. Her hair had escaped from the pins that had held it up, and it was tousled and sexily dishevelled around her shoulders and her naked breasts, her nipples slightly pink and engorged from the heat of his caresses.

He wanted her again. She was like some kind of nymph who could put a spell on him with just a glance, lure him so easily away from rational thoughts. Well, he wasn't going to allow her to control him with her perfectly staged words and her come-hither looks—he'd fallen for that the first time around.

Abbie was aware that the silence between them was stretching tautly. 'We should be getting back to the house now.'

'You're not going anywhere, Abigail…' He pulled her back towards him suddenly and kissed her again. It was a kiss that sent tingles flooding through her entire body.

It was strange how his lips told her one thing, with their seductive, possessive kisses, and his words told her something completely different with their commanding, slightly mocking edge.

The mix set wildly conflicting thought patterns racing through her. Part of her wanted to pull away from him with a toss of her head—part of her wanted to melt into him. She swallowed hard. She didn't want to stop making love with him. The adrenalin was charging through her veins, changing her into somebody she hardly recognised. She hated herself for being so weak.

'Damon, I need to get myself a drink of water.' She pulled away from him abruptly and he let her go, and watched how she pulled her bra up to cover her swollen nipples, before picking up his shirt from the floor and pulling it on to cover her nakedness.

It swamped her, but it also looked incredibly sexy with her stockings and high heels.

He watched her walk away from him towards the kitchen. How was it that just when he thought he had her tamed and submissive she could so easily turn the tables on him? Damon wondered edgily. He got out of bed and threw on a towelling robe that was hanging on the back of the door.

She was pouring herself a glass of water from a bottle she had found in the fridge.

'I'll have one of those while you are there,' he directed softly.

'OK.' She didn't look round at him but reached to get a glass.

'You look good in my shirt, by the way,' he remarked as his eyes moved down over the long length of her legs. 'Even the way it's ripped is strategically enhancing.' He noticed as she turned that he could see the top of her thighs.

She flicked him a slightly nervous glance. She was good at looking at him with just that mixture of uncertainty and desire. It drove him crazy.

'All you need now is the necklace that I bought for you,' he murmured suddenly.

'I told you, Damon, I don't want your gifts.' Her voice trembled slightly.

'Of course you do.' He disappeared for a moment to pick up the jewellery from outside on the patio. Maybe if she wore this hunk of expensive, beautiful stone around her neck it would remind him of what she was, he thought forcefully. Because every time she looked at him in that raw, almost vulnerable way of hers he was in very real danger of forgetting.

'I don't want that necklace, Damon,' she told him softly

when he came back into the kitchen. 'I don't want you to put it anywhere near me.'

'What's the matter, isn't the diamond big enough to satisfy you?' he rasped.

'Don't, Damon!' The look she shot him was so beseeching that it cut.

It would be so easy to forget what she was. She was so gorgeously desirable, all kitten-warmth and come-to-bed eyes.

But he couldn't allow himself to forget…he just couldn't.

'Abbie, I bought this for you as a wedding present, so the least you can do is damn well wear it on our wedding day.'

'Sorry, but I'm not going to.'

'You are so stubborn!'

'So are you!' She glared at him as she walked across towards him with his glass of water. 'You don't listen to me. I don't want your money or your gifts!'

Who the hell did she think she was fooling? he wondered angrily.

'Come here.' He caught hold of her hand as she approached and pulled her towards him. Then, putting down the water on the kitchen bar, he pulled her towards one of the comfortable chairs in the lounge area and brought her down so that she was straddling his knee.

'Now, hold your hair up out of the way.'

She held his gaze with a mutinous stare.

'Do as I ask, Abbie—it's just a necklace.'

'But it's not, is it?' she asked softly. 'It's *not* just a necklace, it's a symbol of what you really think of me.'

He ignored that and opened up the box to take out the necklace. It flashed fire in the sunlight. 'Lift up your hair,' he ordered again.

When she still didn't comply, he placed it around her neck and fastened it over her hair. Then he reached and pulled her hair up, letting it trail through his fingers like liquid gold as he released it.

The chain fell around her neck, the diamond heavy and cold against her skin. He sat back to look at her. 'There… It looks good.'

She hated it, but she left it where it was and just held his gaze defiantly.

'Abbie, don't look at me like that.' There was rawness in his voice for just a second, a note that was at odds with the arrogant dominance of his actions. 'I'll buy you another necklace tomorrow, one that you can choose for yourself, all right?' As he spoke he trailed a hand over her chin, down the line of her neck.

It wasn't all right, but she couldn't speak, her throat felt too choked. She trembled at his touch; she felt so cold inside, yet just the slightest stroke of his hand made her warm again, stirred up a heat she didn't want, couldn't handle, couldn't control.

'Now, where were we?' He started to unfasten the buttons on the shirt, and then as it fell apart he pulled her bra down, exposing her breasts to the darkness of his eyes.

Her heart was thundering painfully against her chest. She wanted him too, so much it hurt.

His fingers played with her nipples, squeezing them, stroking them until they were hard peaks of need. Her hands moved to rest on his thighs, and his fingers became rougher yet inflamed her all the more.

Then suddenly he was inside her, bouncing her on his knee, watching how her breasts moved with each of his thrusts. He put his hands on her slender hips, controlling her, watching how she writhed, how her hair swung silkily around her shoulders, how the diamond sparkled as it nestled between her cleavage.

As she climaxed she called out his name, and he leaned forward and took one breast into his mouth, sucking on her, until he also reached his own climax.

She wrapped her arms around him and buried her face in the dark softness of his hair, holding him tight against her. Her body was convulsed with pleasure, throbbing from the aftermath of a sensation so pleasurable it had exhausted her totally.

They were wrapped so tightly in each other's arms and he was still inside her, still a part of her, so that it was almost as if they had become one.

He stroked her hair back from her face, and as she pulled away from him a little he captured her lips in a dominant, yet tremendously sensual kiss. She wanted it to go on and on, but he pulled away from her after a few moments.

Spent and exhausted, she cuddled in against him.

She tried to remind herself that part of her should still be angry about the necklace—about his dominant, insensitive ways. But try as she might she couldn't rekindle that anger. It felt too good being held by him.

He doesn't trust me—he doesn't love me—but when he's with me like this he is mine…totally mine, she told herself firmly. And for now that was enough, because she loved him so much.

The thought made fear and shock race through her so violently that she shivered.

'Are you OK?'

The concern in his voice caused even greater emotional waves to smash through her body. 'No, not really.' She buried her head into his neck. She couldn't allow herself to be in love with him—he'd never return the feelings, and it hurt too much. And yet she knew now that she was in love with him. Maybe she had never really stopped loving him, and had just tried to persuade herself that she had because it was the only way she'd been able to cope with losing him.

'I didn't hurt you, did I?' He sounded mortified. 'Abbie, I never intended to hurt you.' He gathered her closer, stroking her hair.

She squeezed her eyes tightly closed against the tears that wanted to flow. 'You didn't hurt me. I just had a momentary pang of…something.'

'Of what?' He held her away from him and looked at the bright glitter in her blue eyes. His heart turned over as a tear spilled down over the pallor of her skin.

She shrugged. 'I don't know, I'm being stupid.' She brushed the tears from her eyes harshly and pulled away from him to stand up. She was going to have to pull herself together. She couldn't possibly tell him that she loved him. She remembered his earlier response to her unguarded comment, and she couldn't risk seeing contempt in his eyes now—couldn't risk losing the little pride she had left. 'Maybe I'm just tired. I didn't sleep well last night and, well, it's quite an emotional business getting married, isn't it?'

He frowned. 'I guess it is. Abbie, I—'

'Are you hungry?' She cut across him firmly and smiled. It was the kind of smile that made his heart drum wildly against his chest. The kind of smile that made him question everything he'd done—everything he'd said to her in the last couple of days.

'Because I am,' she continued swiftly. 'I haven't eaten anything all day. I was too tense this morning for breakfast.'

'Were you?' He watched as she pulled his shirt over her curves.

'Of course. Marriage is a big step and, like you, it's something I said I'd never do.'

She moved away from him. In truth she wasn't in the slightest bit hungry, but she needed to do something—needed to change the direction of her thoughts to pull them away from the dangerous edge where they were poised precariously.

She opened the fridge door and looked in. 'There are all sorts of goodies in here—do you want something?'

Damon belted his dressing gown and stood up. Was it his imagination, or was her voice too bright? 'I'll have whatever you are having.'

Abbie brought out some smoked salmon and some salad and put it on the breakfast bar.

'Shall we sit here to eat? I know the table is laid outside, but I just want a snack, and somehow this seems more relaxed.'

'Yes, that's fine.' Damon pulled out one of the breakfast bar-stools and sat opposite her.

The glasses of water from earlier were beside them. 'I'll top these up with ice,' he said as he leaned over to the ice dispenser. 'They might be warm now.'

'Thanks.'

He noticed that she avoided his eyes as he put the glass down beside her again.

Why had she cried? The question burnt through him. Now he thought carefully back over their love-making, he didn't think he'd been rough. She'd seemed to enjoy it, had moaned, with pleasure not pain. Had called out his name with a little husky moan.

Just thinking about it made him want her all over again. How was it that even now, after a wildly passionate afternoon, he still needed her?

He forced himself not to think about that now.

'So you were nervous this morning?' he asked quietly.

'A bit.' She reached for the water and took a long swallow. 'Weren't you?'

There was a moment's silence, and she shook her head. 'Sorry, silly question.'

'It's not a silly question. I had a few last-minute qualms.'

'Really?' She looked at him then.

'I've been a bachelor a long time. Of course I thought deeply about what I was doing this morning.'

She nodded. 'Did you go out last night?' She tried to sound casual, as if she didn't really care what he'd done. But she did care, she cared way, *way* too much about everything.

He shook his head. 'I worked. I had a lot to sort out so I could have a few days off with you now.'

'Oh!' She smiled at him and felt some of the tension inside her easing as he smiled back. He had such a gorgeously sexy smile...

She reached for her glass of water again.

'Thirsty?'

'Yes. I know it's air-conditioned in here, but I feel a bit hot.'

'Again?' He looked at her with a mixture of warmth and humour, and she blushed prettily.

'Well, let me eat something and get my strength back first,' he murmured softly.

She liked the look he slanted across at her, liked the provocatively teasing tone in his voice. It made her sizzle inside.

It was nice sitting here with him like this. If she didn't think too deeply about things, she could pretend that they were just a regular couple—just married and too much in love to keep their hands off each other.

'You know what's missing in here?' he asked suddenly.

'Some music?'

'No, but that could be arranged.' He smiled. 'No, I was talking about the view.'

'You have a spectacular view.' She turned her head to look out the window across the dazzle of the blue sea.

'But it could be better.' He leaned across and unbuttoned the shirt she wore so that he could see the full curves of her body in the lacy bra.

The touch of his hands against her skin made her flare with a deep longing for him.

'And maybe we should get rid of this.'

To her surprise, he reached and unfastened the necklace from around her neck and set it down to one side.

Their eyes held across the table.

Her heart was thundering wildly against her chest as he smiled at her.

'Is that better?' he asked huskily.

She nodded. 'Infinitely better.'

CHAPTER NINE

ABBIE was pretending to read a book as she lay next to the pool, but really she was watching Damon. He was playing in the water with Mario. They'd got some water wings for the child, and he loved being in the pool with his father. He was laughing with delight now as Damon allowed him to kick his legs and make a splash whilst he supported him carefully in strong arms.

She smiled as she watched him raise the child into the air then dip his toes down again in the water, and she loved hearing Mario laugh. She loved watching the muscles ripple powerfully in her husband's arms as he moved. He really had a dreamily wonderful body, she thought distractedly as her eyes moved over his bronzed torso, noticing how his skin gleamed in the bright sunshine.

He looked like he worked out every day. There was a gym down in the basement of the house, but Abbie had never seen him use it. She'd asked him last night as they'd lain together in the deep comfort of their double bed if he ever used it, and he had laughed. 'Not enough hours in the day—anyway, I'm saving all my energy to work out with you.'

They certainly had 'worked out' a lot together this week. Just thinking about it made Abbie's heart race. Since Damon had taken that necklace from around her neck, it was as if they had turned some kind of a corner in their relationship.

She knew nothing had fundamentally changed—deep down he still distrusted her. But it was as if some sort of unspoken truce had occurred, as if a line had been drawn under the past. And Abbie was glad of it, because this had been the most wonderful week of her life. She loved the way Damon could make her feel.

She loved the way he couldn't seem to get enough of her, because she felt exactly the same. Even now, watching him in the pool playing with their son, she wanted him. Yet just a few hours ago he'd taken her back to bed for a siesta. Just thinking about that 'siesta' now made her melt with longing all over again.

She also loved the way he was with Mario, protective and gentle, yet fun. She'd noticed how over the week the little boy had fast grown attached to him, his dark eyes lighting up whenever his father walked into the room.

Damon looked up now and caught her watching him. 'Why don't you come in and join us?'

'No, it's OK, you carry on.' She smiled at him. In truth she didn't want to get too close to him, because she was feeling extremely aroused just watching him. And she didn't want him to know just how much she wanted him *again*.

'Come on, the water is lovely.' He splashed some of it in her direction and the cold hit the heat of her skin, making her jump.

'Ow! It's freezing! I'm definitely not coming in!'

'Don't be such a chicken.' Damon lifted Mario out of the water.

The little boy chuckled as Damon splashed Abbie again.

'Damon, stop!' She swung her long legs over the edge of the sun lounger and put her book down.

Damon's eyes swept over her body with bold approval. She was wearing a very skimpy black-and-white bikini and it looked sensational on her. 'Come into the pool with us,' he said firmly. 'We need you.'

'No, you don't.'

'Yes, *I* do.' He smiled with that half tug of his lips that made her go hot inside.

She watched as he hoisted himself out of the water, his muscles rippling powerfully as they flexed, water gleaming on his broad chest. He slicked his dark wet hair back from his face and grinned at her. 'So are you coming in of your own accord, or do I have to carry you?'

'Don't you dare!'

'Is that a challenge?' He laughed, and before she could say another word he had swept her off her feet and up into his arms. His body was cold against the heat of hers, but he felt so good. She wrapped her arms around his neck.

'Put me down.'

'Amazing how words can say one thing and the body another,' he teased.

'Yes, I often think that about you.'

'Do you? And what is my body saying now, hmm?'

'It's saying, *I adore you, Abigail Cyrenci.*' She whispered the words against his ear. *'And I wouldn't dream of putting you in that cold water…'*

The rest of her words were drowned out as he jumped with her into the pool. Water swished over her head, and the world was a blur as she surfaced, gasping with the shock of the cold.

She glared at him furiously, and he laughed.

'A good cooling-off is just what you needed.'

'That's not what you were saying to me earlier.' She slanted him a provocative look, and he smiled.

'True.'

She pushed her wet hair back off her face, and as she raised her arms it emphasised the firm tilt of her breasts. 'Maybe I'm the one who needs cooling off,' he added gently.

She saw the fire in his eyes, and it lit an answering one deep inside her.

Damon glanced over at Mario, who was happily sitting by the side of the pool playing with some toys. He caught hold of Abbie and turned her until her back was towards the child and pressed against the side of the pool.

'Now, where did we leave off this afternoon, hmm?' He bent his head and kissed her very slowly, very deliberately, on the lips. The sensation was blissful, and she curved her arms around his shoulders and gave herself up to the pleasure.

She could feel his body pressing against hers in the water, could feel the heat of his desire warming her.

One hand moved to pull her bikini top down.

'Damon, someone might see!' Her protest was half-hearted; she was facing the ocean, and she knew there was no one around—besides, she loved the feel of his fingers running over the cool of her skin in the water.

'Who's going to see us?' he murmured with a grin. 'A passing seagull would have difficulty in seeing anything. It's Frederic's day off, Elise is in town, Mario...' Damon's eyes flicked over her shoulder to where the child was busy making a tower out of some plastic bricks '...is otherwise occupied.'

'Even so.' She shivered with need and with pleasure as his fingers found the hard peaks of her nipples.

'Even so, we need to enjoy every moment we can...' He lowered his head and licked at her breast. His tongue was warm against the coldness of her skin and it inflamed her senses wildly.

She leaned her head back against the pool and looked up into the dazzling blue sky, luxuriating in his caresses.

'Because tomorrow I'm back at work.'

'Really?' Her head jerked upwards.

'Yes, really…'

He looked at her with a gleam of amusement in his dark eyes. 'As much as I enjoy taking you to bed morning, noon and night, I've got to get back to reality some time.'

'I suppose.' The words brought a coldness swirling inside to meet the warmth of her desire. She wished he'd said 'making love' and not referred to it as just taking her to bed. She supposed the truth was she really didn't want reality; she liked the dreamy world of desire she had inhabited this last week. What did getting back to reality mean? Was it a return to his cynical manner? Would he be travelling away on business? What would she do all day while she waited for him to come home to her?

'I want you so much…' She whispered the words softly. Her fingers moved tenderly over the strength of his back.

His mouth moved to capture hers, catching her shuddering sighs. His tongue probed her mouth as he pressed against her, invading her senses on every level.

The water swished softly around her body, stroking against it with satin warmth as the sun beat powerfully down.

'You were just getting out of a pool the first time I met you—do you remember?' Damon asked softly as he nuzzled in against her neck.

'Of course I remember.' She closed her eyes as his lips moved upwards towards her ears, the sweet kisses making her shiver with pleasure.

'You looked so beautiful.' He breathed the words against her. 'It was as if you cast some kind of a spell on me that day as you rose out of the water, and I just couldn't get you out of my mind after that—all I could think about was wanting you.'

'I felt the same, Damon,' she whispered tremulously.

He pulled away from her suddenly, his hands leaving her body.

'Damon?' Her eyes met with his. 'I wanted you too…'

Her heart crashed painfully as she noticed that the mocking light was back in the darkness of his eyes. 'And was that before or after your father told you how much money was riding on *wanting* me? Hmm?'

'It wasn't like that.' Her voice shook slightly.

But he wasn't listening, he was moving away from her, swimming with hard, powerful strokes down to the far end of the pool.

Abbie adjusted her swimming costume. She shouldn't have said anything. They couldn't talk about the past—she should know that. But she wished desperately that they could, and that he would know the truth about her feelings and about what had really happened in the past. But trying to cut through his scorn and derision was too hurtful.

She felt pain spiralling through her as she watched him get out of the pool and walk along towards Mario.

With a deep breath, she hoisted herself out of the water and reached for a towel.

'Elise is having a night off tonight.' She tried to keep her voice normal, as if nothing had happened, as if everything was fine and her heart wasn't splintering. She just wanted to put things back to the way they had been earlier.

'Yes, she usually has Sunday off.' Damon reached to take off Mario's armbands. He didn't look up at her. 'We can go into town to eat, if you want—there is a very trendy new bistro you would probably like, and if we go early enough we can bring Mario.'

'Actually, I thought I'd cook dinner for us.'

He glanced up then, and his lips twisted in that cynical way that tormented her so much. 'Can you cook?'

'Yes, actually, I'm a very good cook.' She slanted her chin up defiantly.

He shrugged. 'Well, if you want to make dinner that's fine.'

'Good.' She smiled at him. 'Because I do.'

Mario reached out with a red building-block and handed it to Damon. 'Dada,' he said with a smile.

'Hey, Mario—that's right—Dada.' Abbie crouched down beside the child and smiled at him. She'd been saying 'Daddy' to him a few times this week as she'd handed things over to Damon, but this was the first time he'd said the word himself. 'Clever boy.' She kissed the top of his head, and as she straightened her eyes connected with Damon's. This time there was no hint of mockery in his eyes, just warmth.

Mario's tower toppled over as he tried to put another two bricks on top at the same time.

'Oh dear.' Damon turned to help him pick them up. 'You've got to work at things slowly, Mario. One brick at a time.'

Maybe it was the same with their relationship, Abbie told herself firmly. If she tried really hard and took one minute at a time, one day at a time, then maybe one day there would be a framework for Damon to trust her. She couldn't give up on that hope—she just couldn't.

Damon put some paperwork to one side and glanced at his watch. Abbie had told him that dinner would be at eight, so he'd taken the opportunity to catch up with some work in the study. It was the first he'd done for a week and he really needed to get back into it. He definitely needed to go into his offices in town every day next week, probably some evenings as well.

Trouble was that for the first time in his life he didn't feel driven by work. The overwhelming desire in his heart these days seemed to be spending time with Abbie and Mario.

It was good to feel like that about his son—but his feelings for Abbie were troubling him. She only had to look at him in a certain way—touch him in a certain way—and he was in danger of forgetting the lessons of the past. It was dangerous territory.

But he wasn't a fool, he reminded himself sharply. He knew what she was. And today when she'd tried to pretend that she'd had feelings for him back when they met... Well, he couldn't allow her to think he was falling for that.

He was going to have to watch his emotions carefully. It was probably just as well that work was beckoning. Distance was probably what he needed to think things through.

Damon glanced at his watch again and put away the papers. For now work could wait. He was a bit early for dinner, but he was curious to see how Abbie was getting on. Domesticity wasn't her style. Why she wanted to cook dinner, he didn't know. He could have got someone else in to cater for them, or he could have taken her out and wined and dined her in style. He'd offered both before retiring to his study but she had been adamant.

The clock in the hallway said seven forty-five. He went quietly down towards the kitchen and then stopped by the door through to the dining room. She was standing by the table, lighting some candles. The place looked lovely. She'd lit a fire in the big open-cast fireplace, and laid the table with the best china and silver. Candlelight reflected softly over the polished surface of the table.

As he watched she smoothed a hand almost nervously over her black dress and checked her appearance quickly in one of the large gilt mirrors. She looked stunning, Damon thought as he leaned against the door and watched her with leisurely approval. She was wearing very provocative high heels, and her black dress hugged her slender figure. The square neckline plus the fact that she had put her hair up showed her long neck and her soft curves to full advantage. Her handbag was sitting on the sideboard, and she reached into it and took out a lipstick to apply a red gloss to her lips.

Damon wanted her so much that he ached. He watched as she put the lipstick back into her bag, and he was just about to step into the room to tell her just how much he wanted her when she took out a mobile phone and opened it.

He watched with a frown as she hurriedly started to key in some numbers.

Who was she ringing? he wondered. A part of him wanted to step forward and let her know that he was there, but he didn't. Curiosity rooted him to the spot.

Abbie pulled out a chair and sat down. She had two missed calls on her mobile—both were from the stables. All she could think was that something had happened to her horse. She knew all the business dealings with the stables had to go through Damon now, but Jess knew how much Benjo meant to her and if there was something wrong she would want to tell her per-sonally.

It seemed to take for ever before someone picked up the phone. It was Jess and she sounded out of breath as if she'd just dashed in from outside.

'Hi, it's Abbie here. Have you been trying to ring me?'

'Yes… Oh, Abbie, I'm so sorry!'

The genuine distress in the other woman's voice struck horror into her. There *was* something wrong with her horse!

'It's your father.'

The words stilled Abbie's mind.

'He's been here, and he's been insisting I give him your mobile phone number—he wouldn't go away. I know you don't want to talk to him, Abbie, but in the end I had to give it to him, and I had to tell him where you were. He was—bullish.'

'I can imagine,' Abbie said dryly. She closed her eyes. At least it wasn't as bad as she had thought. She'd rather deal with a few phone calls from her father than hear that something had happened to her horse. 'Don't worry about it. I'll sort it out. How's Benjo?'

'He's in good form. We all miss you here, Abbie. But the stables are fine; you don't need to worry about them. How's Mario?'

'He's well—fast asleep, tucked up in his cot. We miss you too.'

The clock out in the hallway struck eight and Abbie remembered about dinner. 'Listen, I've got to go.'

'OK—and I am sorry, Abbie. I feel like I've let you down, giving your father that information, but honestly I had no choice. Oh, and after I told him where you were he rang someone called Lawrence.'

'Lawrence Woods,' Abbie murmured uncomfortably. She had hoped she'd never have to hear that name again. He was her father's very dodgy accountant.

'That's right, and he told him where you were and talked about some business deal.'

Abbie pushed a hand tiredly through her hair and wondered what her father was up to. Why couldn't he just leave her alone? 'Did he say what the deal was?'

'No, just that he was sure it would be in the bag now.'

'Don't worry about it.' Abbie tried to lighten her tone to make Jess feel better. 'I'll sort it out. No problem.'

'I hope so. That man is a bully.'

'I know. But I also know how to handle him. You take care, and keep in touch.'

As the connection was cut, Abbie's false bravado also died. The last thing she wanted was to deal with her father.

She sat quietly for a few moments, trying to pull herself

together, then she got quietly up from the table and pushed the chair back in. John Newland couldn't hurt her any more, she told herself fiercely. He was miles away, and she'd do what she had done in St Lucia and just ignore his calls.

'So…how is dinner going, Abbie?'

The voice from the doorway made her whirl around. Damon was standing there watching her.

'Fine.' She smiled at him, but he didn't smile back; he was watching her with deep, unfathomable eyes. 'I didn't hear your footsteps,' she said nervously. 'How long have you been standing there?'

'Not long.' One dark eyebrow lifted quizzically. 'Have you been on the phone?'

She hesitated for just a moment, wondering if he'd heard her. Then she realised he'd asked her because she was still holding her mobile in her hand. Even so, for a split second she debated telling the truth—and then she panicked. Her father was such an explosive subject between them, and things were shaky enough without any reminders of the past casting even more shadows. Besides, why let John Newland ruin a perfectly nice evening?

'I was just…checking my messages.'

Damon watched with a frown as she went to drop her phone back into her bag. And he knew exactly why she was lying.

At first he'd thought her conversation had sounded banal enough. He'd presumed, because she'd asked about a horse, that she was just talking to someone at the stables.

But then she had mentioned a name that had brought a red-hot wave of fury sweeping over him: *Lawrence Woods*. Damon remembered that name very well. Lawrence Woods was the accountant John Newland had used to help rip off his father in Vegas. He was her father's right-hand henchman.

And then she had asked what the deal was.

John Newland didn't do a deal without his crooked accountant. *She'd been talking to her father.*

The very thought turned his stomach. But the more Damon thought about it the more likely it was. Things had moved pretty fast since he had last seen Newland, and he'd probably been out to the stables looking for his daughter.

And he was probably very impatient to learn what kind of financial deal she had cut. He was probably looking for some money to invest in one of his shady deals.

Damon advanced further into the room. 'And were there any messages?'

She turned, and for a second he glimpsed a decidedly uneasy light in her blue eyes. 'No, nothing. Now I really had better get back into the kitchen.' She smiled up at him. 'Why don't you sit down, make yourself comfortable?'

But Damon didn't sit down, and as she walked over towards the door he was blocking her way, looking at her with those dark eyes in a way that made her very apprehensive.

She looked up at him questioningly. 'Is everything OK?'

'You tell me, Abbie.'

The grating, sardonic tone disconcerted her completely. 'Yes. I just need to turn the oven off...'

Still he didn't move out of her way.

On impulse she reached up and touched his face softly, then stood on tiptoe to kiss his cheek. He made no attempt to touch her, and that took her aback. Usually if she kissed him he would kiss her back, touch her. 'I want us to just relax and enjoy tonight.' Did she sound as tense as she suddenly felt?

Of course, he should have realised immediately that she was up to something when she'd offered to cook for him, Damon thought wryly. After all, he'd already heard via the grapevine that John Newland was searching around for money, trying to set up a shady business deal with an old associate of his. Abbie probably wanted to invest—she'd probably been re-assuring her father that she would be able to siphon money away from her new rich husband to send to him.

The more he thought about it, the more obvious it was. There had to be something in it for her. That was why she'd been suddenly so keen to cook him dinner. That was why she was looking up at him so seductively. Abbie wasn't the domestic type, but she was the seductive, temptress type who knew how to use every feminine wile in the book to get what she wanted. She'd proved that long ago.

Rage started to pound through him.

'Damon?' Her hands moved to rest on his chest, and she looked up at him, perplexed by the fact that he still hadn't made any attempt to either move out of her way or pull her closer and kiss her.

'So tell me, Abbie, what's this really all about?' he asked quietly.

'Sorry?' She frowned. 'I don't know what you mean.'

'I mean this.' He nodded towards the beautifully laid table. 'What was really running through that pretty head of yours as you lit those candles and played at being Ms Domesticated, hmm?'

The mocking tone made colour flare in her cheeks, and her hands dropped from his chest. 'I wasn't playing at anything. I told you, I want us to have a nice relaxing evening—after all, we are still officially on our honeymoon.'

His heart drummed ferociously against his chest. Her acting abilities were too good. But then of course that shouldn't come as any surprise to him; he'd experienced her acting skills before. He remembered how easily she had convinced him that she was vulnerable and shy as she'd given herself to him that first time in Palm Springs. Would he never learn where she was concerned? He didn't know whom he was angrier with—

himself for ever questioning the truth about her when he had held her in his arms, or her for being the gold-digging hussy that she undoubtedly was.

'You know, Abbie, if you want something you don't need to go to these great lengths. I've told you, you can have anything you wish for. All I ask is that you follow the terms of our agreement. And it goes without saying that I want you to have no contact with your father, and certainly no involvement in his shady deals.'

The sudden blunt statement took her very much by surprise, and it hurt. 'I've told you, Damon, I don't want anything from you!' She tried to pull away from him, but he put his hands on her waist suddenly and held her firm.

Her eyes burned as she looked up at him. 'Damon, I can assure you that I've had no contact with my father.'

'Just like you assured me that you were just checking the messages on your phone a few moments ago?' he demanded tersely. 'I know you were lying to me, Abbie. I heard you talking.'

He watched as her face drained of colour.

'So, are you going to tell me what it's all about?' he asked lazily.

'There's nothing to tell.' She was furious that he had tried to catch her out like this.

'Really?' Damon's tone was scathing. 'So, if it was such an innocuous phone call, why lie about it?'

'Because I didn't want to ruin our evening together!' She looked up at him, and for a moment her eyes shimmered with feeling. 'You always like to think the worst of me, don't you?'

His gaze held with hers steadily. 'I'd just prefer it if you didn't try to pretend, Abbie.'

'I wasn't pretending about anything.' She bit down on her lip. 'The phone call wasn't worth mentioning.'

'But worth lying about.'

'Because you never trust me!' The cry broke from her lips. 'Why can't you just trust me?'

Damon watched her, his eyes dark, cold and uncompromising. He wasn't going to be drawn in by her plea, or by the beauty of her eyes. He'd been stupid to ever doubt himself where she was concerned. She could lie her way out of anything. 'Why should I trust you?' he asked coldly. 'I only married you because you are the mother of my son—and also for your body, of course. "To have and to hold" I think was the deal…nothing more.'

The words shouldn't have come as any great surprise. She knew what the deal was, she knew how he felt. Yet after their week of glorious love-making they struck her as painfully as if he'd physically hit her. She had dared to hope that he was softening towards her, that if she was patient he would perhaps start to see her in a different light, but she knew now how stupid those dreams had been.

'So, let's drop the pretence, hmm?' he suggested now.

She shrugged. 'If that's how you want things.' Her voice was numb.

'It is.' He dropped his hands from her waist. 'Now, run along and see to whatever it was you were doing in the kitchen before you burn the house down.'

Anger shot to her own defence. 'If the house burns down it will be your fault, not mine.' How dared he talk to her like this? Who did he think he was?

She marched past him, glad to escape into the kitchen, but to her consternation Damon followed her and lounged against the door, watching as she moved towards the oven to turn it off.

'So, tell me about the phone call,' he demanded. 'And I don't want to hear any more lies.'

'Go to hell, Damon.'

'I want to know exactly what you were planning, Abbie.'

'I wasn't planning anything. And I certainly wasn't speaking to my father! We haven't spoken in over two years!' Almost before she could finish what she was saying, she heard her mobile phone ringing again in the next room.

'Well, well, I wonder who that could be?' Damon asked sarcastically, and watched as her skin once more flooded with colour. 'What's the betting, if I go and answer that, it will be Newland again with some instruction he forgot to give you?'

Abbie shook her head, but she couldn't find her voice to answer, because she was terrified that it could very well be her father, and Damon would never believe that she hadn't solicited the call. 'I don't take instructions from my father,' she managed shakily instead.

'Of course not.' Damon's tone was cynical. 'But it could be him?'

She shrugged helplessly.

'So, shall I answer it for you?' He made as if to turn away, and her eyes widened anxiously.

'No! Don't, Damon—please!'

He turned back slowly. 'So now we are getting to the truth.'

To Abbie's relief the phone suddenly stopped ringing. 'I suppose he wants money for some deal,' Damon said tensely into the ensuing silence. 'I had heard he was up to his old tricks.'

'I don't know what he is up to. I don't want anything to do with him.' She raised her chin and met his eyes steadily. 'And that is the truth.'

'You really are a great actress, Abbie.' Damon's lips twisted with bitter amusement.

He was never going to believe anything she said, Abbie realised dully. And could she blame him after what had happened in the past? She turned away from him, and tried to busy herself taking the dinner from the oven, but she felt like she was just running on some kind of automatic pilot. She didn't care about dinner now, and there was a knot of pain inside her that just wouldn't go away, no matter how she tried to swallow it down.

Damon watched as she bent over and took out the last of the dishes. He was furious with her, yet at the same time through the mist of his fury he couldn't help noticing how her skirt rode up as she crouched down to pick something up. Then she smoothed a hand over her dress as she straightened, and he found his attention wandering down over the soft curves of her figure.

She was an enticing witch, he thought, raking a hand through the thick darkness of his hair. But he'd known that from day one this time around, he reminded himself fiercely. Any weakness that he had felt for her as she had looked up at him with those kitten eyes had been entirely his own stupidity.

Of course she would be conniving with her father if she got the chance—that was what she did. *He knew that*.

All he could do was watch her carefully, and stick to his original plan—use her the way she had once used him.

'So what is on the menu tonight?' he asked suddenly as she straightened up and put the trays out on the racks to cool.

She shot him a look of uncertainty. 'I decided I would try some Sicilian recipes,' she told him tremulously. 'And I asked Elise what you liked.'

'Really?' Damon shook his head. 'I have to say that, even though I know it's just one of your little ploys, I like the idea, and you do suit the guise of the domestic goddess.'

She closed her eyes and tried to cut out the mocking scorn of his voice. 'It wasn't a ploy. I wanted tonight to be special.'

'You can still do something special for me.' His voice held a commanding, sensual edge that wasn't lost on her.

She bit down on her lip and shook her head. If he touched her she felt sure she would break down.

'Come here.'

'Damon, I—'

'Come here, Abbie,' he cut across her firmly, and after a moment's hesitation she did as he asked, stopping at arm's length from him.

'Don't ever lie to me again.' His voice rasped harshly as he reached out and pulled her closer. He put a hand under her chin, tipping her face so that she was forced to look up at him.

'You belong to me now, Abbie, body and soul. Don't forget that.'

How could she forget it when even the lightest touch of his hand against her face was like a burning brand of possession making her whole body tremble with longing?

He leaned closer and kissed her. There was anger in his kiss, but it was also searing, and achingly passionate. Before she could stop herself she was moving closer and responding. How could he give her so much pleasure and at the same time stir up so much pain inside her? she wondered hazily.

She hated the things he said to her, yet she still wanted him, she still loved him. She hated herself for her weakness.

She felt his hand hitching up her dress.

'Do you want to go upstairs?' She whispered the words breathlessly as need overtook all other emotions.

'No.' He found the lace of her knickers and pulled them down, then turned her around towards the kitchen counter. 'I want you here.'

CHAPTER TEN

DAMON stared up into the darkness of the bedroom. He hadn't been able to get enough of Abbie last night. He'd taken her ruthlessly, and she had responded totally to him, her fire matching his ardour.

And once upstairs the same thing had happened all over again. He'd taken her with a cold-blooded determination, as if trying to purge the need he felt for her. Yet the strange thing was that, no matter how many times he took her, that need was still alive.

He thought about the way she had given herself to him— that shy look in her eyes, and then the fiery, wild, uncontrolled way she had responded to him as he'd kissed her.

Afterwards she had taken a shower in the *en-suite* bathroom and had returned wearing a white satin nightdress. She'd looked so pure in it, her face fresh and scrubbed of make-up, and her blond hair lying in loose, glossy curls around her shoulders. Oh yes, she'd been the picture of beautiful innocence, which went to show how deceptive looks could be, he thought with a wry twist of his lips.

'Take the nightgown off,' he had murmured as she had reached the side of the bed.

'Damon, do you have to be so cold with me?'

She had sat down at the edge of the bed and looked at him with an underlying sadness in her eyes that had torn him up inside. Just thinking about it now made his stomach clench. He didn't know what bothered him more—the anger he felt for still allowing the way she looked at him to affect him, or her for playing her games so damn well.

When he'd made no reply she had taken the nightdress off, her eyes holding with his gaze, her chin tipped up so that there'd been a hint of defiance about her acquiescence. Then, as she'd slipped into the bed beside him, she had been the one to reach for him.

She'd rolled over on top of him and had looked into his eyes before kissing him deeply, opening her mouth and allowing him inside. 'I wasn't lying to you earlier, Damon. But you've proved your point,' she had whispered softly. 'I'm yours totally.'

She rolled over in the bed now, and he felt the warmth of her body against him. The soft sincerity of those words had plagued him all night. A part of him hated himself for taking her body the way he had. If she'd tried to pull back from him he would have stopped, but she had given herself so freely...so lovingly. He frowned.

She had given herself freely and lovingly in Palm Springs too, he reminded himself angrily. She was a con artist.

Dawn was breaking outside now, and the first rays of sunshine started to slant across the room. He turned on his side and looked down at Abbie, and impulsively he stroked a stray strand of hair away from her face so that he could see her more clearly.

Her skin was perfect; her lashes were long and dark, and her lips infinitely kissable. There was almost an ethereal loveliness about her, a delicate-rose vulnerability.

But of course all roses had very sharp thorns, he reminded himself tersely. But she was achingly beautiful...

Her eyes flickered open suddenly and connected with his. 'What time is it?' she murmured sleepily.

'Almost six.'

'You're awake early.' As she slowly focussed, memories from the night before came flooding back: Damon taking her again and again, his attitude demanding and ruthless. Yet just now as their eyes had met there had been something else. She frowned as she tried to place the expression in the darkness of his eyes. Regret?

'I've got to go into the office early.' He rolled away from her onto his back.

She didn't want him to go. More than anything she just wanted him to reach out to her and put an arm around her, wanted to close out the harsh memories of last night and the demanding way he had taken her body. Maybe he wanted that too. Maybe he regretted his coldness.

'Do you have to go?' she ventured softly. 'We could spend the day together, and—'

'I don't think so,' he cut across her firmly. 'I need to make sure my businesses are ticking along smoothly. And, anyway, I'm sure you'd rather I got my priorities straight—you don't want the money to dwindle, do you, Abbie? You wouldn't like that.'

She closed her eyes against the pain stirred up by those sizzling, scornful words. So much for him regretting anything! 'Don't, Damon,' she whispered huskily.

'I'm just being practical.' That was the way he had to be around her, he told himself forcefully. 'Why don't you go shopping today? Your credit card has arrived. You just need to sign it.'

'There's nothing I need.'

'I'm sure you'll think of something.'

The hard edge to his tone hurt. She took a deep breath and

tried to pull herself together, tried to face up to the reality of her life. She needed to stop lying to herself and recognise the truth: Damon would never love her; their marriage was purely a convenience for him. He'd made that abundantly clear even in the way he had taken her body last night.

He had pleasured himself callously with her and yet, through all of that, she had imagined she had tasted something in his kiss—something more than just raw sexual need.

It was known as 'grasping at straws', she told herself now scornfully. Or maybe she had just been trying to excuse the way she had responded to him.

'What time will you be home tonight?' she asked softly.

'I don't know, Abbie. I'll be late.'

'Fine.' She frowned and swallowed hard.

Something in the tone of her voice made him look over at her again. 'Go and have some fun spending money on yourself, Abbie. The credit limit on your card is high, and—'

'I don't want to spend your money, Damon!' she cut across him furiously. 'Why won't you ever listen to me? I want to spend time getting to know you, I want...' She trailed off as she realised that it didn't matter what she wanted. She was just grasping at more straws.

'You want to spend time getting to know me?' He leaned up on his elbow to look at her better. He sounded very amused now, and that annoyed her. 'What exactly do you want to know?'

'I don't know...everything.' She shrugged. 'You could take me on a tour of the island. Show me where you grew up.' She threw the suggestion at him wildly.

He laughed. 'And you'd be disappointed.'

'Why?'

'Well, my old family home would probably tick all your

boxes, I suppose, although it needs a lot of work doing to it as it's been empty a long time. But I only actually lived there until the age of eight.' He rolled over onto his back again. 'My father lost everything at that point and we had to move. I don't think you would be in the slightest bit interested to see where I lived for the next ten years. It was a bit of a slum area, to be honest.'

'So your father had lost everything once before?' She looked at him in surprise.

'Yes, and then made it all back. Bought back his old house. Only to lose it all again in Vegas. Bizarre, isn't it?' Damon stared up at the ceiling. 'He was a bit of a gambler. Not in the cards-and-horses sense, but in an entrepreneurial way. He liked to take risks in business. You'd think he'd have learnt first time around, that when something seems too good to be true it generally is.'

'So your mum left him when he lost all his money first time around?'

'Yes. I don't suppose he was easy to live with, and my mother—well, my mother likes luxury.'

'Likes? Is she still alive?' For some reason Abbie had assumed his mother was dead.

'Oh yes, she's in the south of France now, I believe. Hooked herself another millionaire and got married again about three years ago.' There was silence for a moment. 'I can understand her leaving my father. Living with someone who takes risks all the time can be hard. But he was a good man in other ways.'

Abbie sat up a little to look at him, and saw the shadows of pain for just a fleeting second in the darkness of his eyes. His childhood must have been tough, she thought with sympathy. She could understand a woman leaving her husband, but not her child. And she guessed Damon had had trouble accepting that too. No wonder he was so determined to give Mario a secure upbringing. Damon saw the expression of concern in her eyes. 'You don't need to worry,' he grated sardonically. 'I don't take wild gambles in business.'

'I wasn't worried.'

'No?' One dark eyebrow lifted in disbelief. 'Well, you can rest assured, the risks I take are all very well calculated.'

'I know that already, Damon. Your risks are calculated in marriage as well as in business.'

He didn't say anything to that.

She wondered if she had inadvertently struck Damon's Achilles' heel. Maybe, because of his mother, he thought most women were more interested in money than love, and his theory had been compounded by what had happened between them in Vegas.

Mario was waking up in the next room. Abbie could hear him happily talking to himself, but she didn't move immediately to go to see to him. It was the first time that Damon had ever opened up to her about his past and she didn't want to lose the moment. 'I would be interested to see where you lived, Damon, both before and after things went wrong in your parents' marriage.'

For a second he looked at her with an odd expression in his eyes. Then he shook his head. 'Maybe another day.'

He pulled away from her and pushed back the duvet. 'I've got to shower and get to work. And it sounds like our son needs his breakfast.'

She watched as he disappeared into the bathroom. Then with a sigh she reached for her dressing gown. The precious shared intimacies had been nothing more than illusion. The reality was that Damon probably regretted telling her anything.

Damon left for the office half an hour later, and Abbie, bathed and dressed in a skimpy pair of shorts and a T-shirt, carried Mario to the front door to wave him goodbye.

Although it was early, the air was already shimmering with heat. It promised to be another scorching day, and Damon felt a frisson of reluctance as he got into his limo and glanced back at the perfect tableaux of his wife and son framed in the doorway.

Abbie looked so beautiful and so young. He forgot sometimes that she was only twenty-one, because in some ways she was so mature for her years. But everything about her was deceptive, he reminded himself forcefully—she knew how to play innocent so well.

As Frederic drove along the twisting, mountainous roads, Damon took out some files and his mobile phone to try and get ahead with some work. He had several intense meetings lined up for this afternoon, and needed to get a handle on things well before then.

But somehow the columns of figures he was supposed to be studying seemed to blur as he read them, and his mind seemed to wander. He was remembering the way Abbie had curled in beside him this morning.

I would be interested to see where you lived, Damon, both before and after things went wrong in your parents' marriage.

The words teased him provocatively. Of course, it was all part of her act. She would be horrified to see where he had grown up. After his father had divorced, he had ploughed all the money he could back into starting again in business. Corners had been cut—and living accommodation had been one of those corners.

However, experiencing that poverty had strengthened Damon's character. Everything he had achieved in life, he'd worked for. Abbie wouldn't understand that—wouldn't be interested, even.

So why had she seemed so interested?

He frowned and tried to return his concentration to his papers.

Women like Abbie lived for shopping and luxury; they didn't want to delve too deeply into anything else.

So why hadn't she just grabbed her credit card and headed happily into town this morning?

Her words played through his mind over and over… *I don't want to spend your money, Damon! Why won't you ever listen to me? I want to spend time getting to know you…*

Damon frowned and closed the words out. She was just clever, that was all. She believed in playing the bigger game—she wanted cash to invest in her father's schemes, not a credit card that could be checked on.

The traffic increased as they approached the outskirts of town.

But she hadn't actually asked him for any cash, he reminded himself suddenly. Well, not *yet*.

And she had looked at him with such feeling in her eyes when she had come to his bed last night. He found himself remembering how he had taken her again. He remembered how pale her skin had looked against the dark-granite worktops in the kitchen. Then he found himself remembering again how she had looked in the white-satin nightdress.

I wasn't lying to you… Her tremulous whisper replayed in his mind.

Why the hell was he thinking about that? Of course she was lying—and why should he take any kind of risk on her? A marriage of convenience just suited him fine. She was good in bed and she was a good mother to Mario. That was all that mattered to him.

Your risks are calculated in marriage as well as in business.

He frowned as he remembered those words. She had a point.

The feelings Abbie had generated in him the first time around in Vegas had troubled him even before he'd found out exactly what she was up to. Because he didn't trust easily—he never had. Marrying Abbie on his terms, cutting away the emotion and just making it a practical arrangement, had suited him. She was right about that.

The truth of that sat uncomfortably with him.

They were gridlocked in traffic now. It looked as if there had been an accident up ahead.

Damon leaned forward and opened up the partition between him and his driver. 'It looks like we are going to be stuck here for a while, Frederic. Turn the car around.'

'You want to find a way around this?'

'No. Just take me back to the house.' Damon frowned. He needed to find his way around the thoughts plaguing him before anything else.

Abbie felt lost when Damon left. She stood on the doorstep for a few moments and watched as the car disappeared from sight.

Then she returned to the kitchen to give Mario his break-fast. Elise was already there, and the two women chatted as Abbie sat down to spoon-feed Mario his cereal. The little boy seemed more interested in playing with the food rather than eating it, and he wasn't happy when she took the spoon away from him.

The shrill ring of the doorbell took them both by surprise.

'I'll go and see who it is. Won't be a moment.' Elise put the bread she had been making into the oven and hurried out. She returned a few moments later, and Abbie could hear her talking to someone in English.

She frowned, wondering who it could be. Then she heard a familiar male voice that made her heart freeze.

'Yes, I've just flown in this morning. I have some business here, so I thought I'd drop by and say hello.'

The kitchen door swung open. 'Abbie, it's your father.' Elise led the man in with a smile. 'That's a nice surprise, isn't it…?' Her cheerful words trailed away as she saw the shock on Abbie's face.

'Hello, sweetheart.' The drawled words held a veiled sarcasm that wasn't lost on his daughter.

She hadn't seen John Newland since she had fled from Vegas a few months before Mario had been born. But he hadn't changed much. He'd never been what you would term attractive. Due to his love of excessive living he was a portly man, and he looked older than his fifty years, with greying hair and sharp eyes. He was dressed for business in a grey suit and looked like he'd just stepped out of his office.

'Shall I make a pot of tea?' Elise ventured gently into the silence.

'No thank you, Elise, my father won't be staying.' From somewhere Abbie managed to find the strength to get to her feet.

'Of course I'm staying—I want to see my grandson. Don't worry, I have plenty of time,' John contradicted her firmly, and then turned to Elise with a charming smile. 'But perhaps you'd give us a few moments alone? I haven't seen my daughter for a while and we parted on, well, unfortunate terms.'

'Unfortunate terms?' Abbie was incensed, and her voice was sharp with disgust. 'It was a lot more than that!'

'You obviously have things to talk about and need some privacy,' Elise said quickly. And before Abbie could say anything to the contrary she left them.

'Nice place you've got yourself here.' John walked further into the room. 'You've done well.'

It spoke volumes that all her father was concerned about was the wealth of her surroundings. He had hardly even glanced at his grandchild.

'You've got a nerve, coming here.'

'I think I've got every right to come here,' he replied calmly. 'And, well, frankly I expected a bit more gratitude than that.'

'Gratitude?' Abbie's voice rose slightly. 'Why on earth would I be grateful to you? All you've ever tried to do is ruin my life, like you ruined my mother's.'

'Not that tired old refrain.' John shook his head. 'Change the record, Abbie. If it wasn't for me you wouldn't have any of this.' He spread his hands out to indicate the house. 'I was the one who prompted Damon into doing the right thing by you. I suspected he'd take the bait. He always did like to think he was the honourable type—they are always quite easy to sucker.'

'He *is* the honourable type. You haven't suckered anybody!' Abbie moved to the back door and opened it. 'I want you to go. You are not welcome here.'

'Now now, Abbie, that's not very respectful!' Instead of moving to the door, he sat down in the chair she had vacated and looked at Mario. 'So this is the heir apparent. He looks like his father.'

'Just get away from him.'

Mario reached out a hand and smiled at his granddad, and Abbie watched with a stab of horror as her father took the little hand in his. 'Hello, little fellow.'

'Get away from him!' She stepped back into the room to pick him up, but her father stopped her by standing up and placing himself in front of the child.

'I'm just saying hello to my grandson. There is no need for these hysterics.'

'You haven't come to say hello. You haven't been interested enough to even bother enquiring after him until now.'

'Well, I tried to ring you just before you left St Lucia, Abbie, and you didn't take my calls.'

'You wonder why?' Her eyes glared stonily into his.

'Come on, Abbie, things don't have to be like this between us.'

He put a conciliatory hand on her arm, and she shook it away angrily. 'What do you want?'

'Well, like I said, I think a little gratitude is in order for setting you up here so well. You know I've always had your best interests at heart.'

Abbie stared at him, nonplussed. 'Best interests at heart? You blackmailed me into going along with your vicious deal in Vegas—told me that you wouldn't pay for Mum's treatment in hospital unless I did what you asked. You got me implicated in something that ruined Damon's father financially, a ploy that tore our relationship apart, and you think I should show you gratitude?'

'Well, you're happy now, aren't you? It all worked out for the best.'

'No, it did not work out for the best!' Abbie blazed with fury. 'I can't believe you are saying this! I knew you were evil, but I didn't think you were mad. You tried to ruin my life!'

'You know what? You sound just like your mother,' her father spat contemptuously.

'Good, because I loved my mother.'

'Don't I just know it—you made a laughing stock of me when you encouraged her to leave!'

'And you never forgave me, did you? But she needed to get out from under your thumb. You made her deeply unhappy with your womanizing, and—'

'Let's just cut to the bottom line, shall we?' John Newland sliced across her in a bored tone. 'I'm currently in the middle of some business negotiations that are doing well—but as you know, thanks to your husband, I am a little bit strapped for cash.'

'You've come here for money?'

'Yes. I've been talking to Lawrence, and he thinks a nice, round five-figure sum should get the deal in the bag…' John mused for a moment before naming his sum exactly.

Abbie stared at him in shock. 'I haven't got any money, and even if I had I wouldn't give you a single penny.'

'I think your attitude is a little unreasonable, Abbie. After all, we are partners in this…marriage arrangement. I suggested it—I told you how to play it. I set the ball rolling by sending Damon to you. I think the least you can do is settle your account.'

'I'm not partners with you in anything. I never have been and I never will be. And I haven't spoken to you since my mother died over two years ago!'

'I was hoping you were going to take a more realistic line than this.' John shook his head. 'I could make your life very uncomfortable here, Abbie. I could stir things up with a lot of force. Damon believed me once before, when I told him you were my willing partner in that deal involving his father. He swallowed it hook, line and sinker when I told him you are nothing but a little gold-digger. I could throw a few more curve-balls into his mind. A few telephone conversations—a few well-placed remarks.'

Abbie knew he was right. One well-worded sentence was all it would take to ruin her fragile marriage. That much had been more than obvious last night.

'All I need is that money then I'll be out of your hair.' Her father's tone was wheedling now. 'You won't see me again.'

'Until the next time there's some big deal and you need some more money,' Abbie answered quietly. She loved Damon, and she didn't want her marriage to fail, but she couldn't do this. 'As I told you, I don't have any money, but even if I had I wouldn't pay you a penny. You've blackmailed me once and I won't let you do it again.'

John Newland looked genuinely taken aback.

'Go—do your worst, dad. I'll take my chances with Damon.'

'You're not thinking this through.'

'On the contrary, my thinking has never been clearer.' A noise from behind them both made Abbie turn, and she froze with shock as she saw Damon standing in the open doorway. His features were grim as his eyes moved from her towards her father, and he looked truly menacing.

'Well,' he drawled. 'Look what's crawled out from under a stone.'

John Newland turned to face him. 'Nice to see you too,' he said in a falsely bright tone. But Abbie could see that, although he tried to sound as if he wasn't intimidated, he shrank a little as Damon took a step forward.

'Damon, this…this isn't what it looks like!' Abbie's voice was distraught. How much had Damon heard? He looked so angry—maybe he thought she had invited her father here. If that was the case, her marriage really was over.

'Get out of my house, Newland.'

'You can't throw me out. I have a right to be here.' John tried to pull himself up to his full height and face Damon down, but his voice wasn't steady. 'This is my daughter and my grandson.'

'No, this is *my* wife and *my* son. Now get out of here, before I call the police and have you arrested for trespassing.'

'Don't be ridiculous! You are making a big mistake…' For just a moment her father blustered. 'Abbie invited me here—'

'No, *you've* made the big mistake,' Damon grated, and as he took another purposeful step closer her father turned and ran for the door.

As soon as he'd gone, Abbie sank down onto the chair in shocked reaction. Her legs were shaking and she felt sick.

'I didn't invite him, Damon, I didn't!'

Damon didn't reply. He just stood by the door. She noticed his hands clenching and unclenching at his sides as if he was trying to get a grip on his emotions.

'You don't believe me, do you?' She covered her face with her hands. After last night and the phone call, he probably assumed she was indeed back in business with her father.

Mario started to cry suddenly, long, wailing sobs that brought Abbie instantly back to her feet. 'It's OK, darling.' She bent to look at the child and then, as she picked him up to comfort him, Damon walked past her and out of the room.

'Damon, we need to talk—' she called after him, but he'd gone, and a few minutes later she heard the front door closing.

CHAPTER ELEVEN

ABBIE had wanted to run after Damon, grab hold of him and beg him to listen. But instead she had stood immobilised until she had heard him driving away.

It was now nearly three in the afternoon and he hadn't come back. He was either still furiously angry with her or else he didn't care and was just carrying on with his work. Either way, any hope she had of making this marriage work was now effectively over, she realised with a heavy heart.

Even if he had stayed and talked to her, it wouldn't have made any difference. Damon would never believe that she hadn't invited her father to this house. He probably thought that the moment he'd left for work this morning she had been on the phone to him again, and that she was hatching some plot with him.

Mario was crying again. He'd been fractious all day, and hadn't settled at all to have his afternoon nap. She went to see him now and lifted him out of the cot.

'It's OK, darling,' she whispered softly to him, and buried her face against his. She felt like crying the way he was crying, giving in to loud, noisy sobs. But that wasn't going to solve anything.

He was very hot, she noticed. Maybe he was teething. She

reached for his soother and put it to his lips to see if it would help, but he pushed it away.

'You are out of sorts, aren't you, Mario?' Abbie pressed a kiss to his cheek. 'Come on, let's give up on sleep and go downstairs and sit quietly, see if we can settle you.'

But, down in the lounge, Mario seemed even more restless.

Elise came into the room as she heard his wails. 'This isn't like Mario,' she said with concern.

'No. I don't know what's wrong with him. I thought he was teething, but I think it's more than that now.' She put a hand to his forehead. 'He's running a bit of a temperature. I think I should make an appointment with the doctor for him. Just have him checked over to be on the safe side.'

'Yes, it might be best.' Elise nodded. 'Do you want me to ring up and make the appointment? Signor Cyrenci's doctor's number is on the diary in the study.'

Abbie nodded. 'If you don't mind, Elise, just in case I have any difficulties with the language.'

'No problem.' Elise bustled away and was back a few moments later. 'All fixed for half-past four this afternoon. Is that OK with you?'

'Yes, great, thank you.' Abbie was trying to put a cooling cloth to Mario's face but he kept pushing it away.

'Do you think we should ring Signor Cyrenci?' Elise asked suddenly. 'Tell him that Mario isn't well?'

'He's probably dealing with important business,' Abbie responded rawly, then thought better of the reply. She was angry and hurt with Damon for just walking out on her, for not caring enough to even talk to her about what had happened— for not loving her.

But he did love his son. And there would be nothing more important to him than Mario's welfare. 'But maybe you'd better ring him,' she added softly. 'I'd probably get his secretary who can't speak English or something…'

'Not if you phoned him direct on his mobile.' Elise picked up Abbie's phone, which was sitting next to her on the table, and passed it over.

She hesitated for a moment before taking it. It wasn't that she didn't want to speak to Damon—it was more a case of being afraid of speaking to him, afraid of losing the last shreds of her dignity and breaking down whilst he remained unmoved and uncaring. She didn't think she could bear that.

But this wasn't about them, this was about Mario, she reminded herself staunchly as she took the phone.

Elise smiled at her, and then reached to take Mario from her. 'I'll look after him for you while you do that.'

Even though she was left alone and in silence, it took Abbie several minutes to gather up the courage to make the call.

Damon answered almost immediately, and before he could say anything she took a deep breath and launched straight in.

'I wouldn't have rung you at work, only there's a problem with Mario and I thought I'd better let you know.' She heard the cold note in her voice, but she couldn't take it out. And why should she, anyway? He didn't care about her.

'What kind of a problem?' Immediately Damon sounded concerned.

'He's been crying all day and he's running a temperature. I've had to get an appointment for him with your GP.'

'What time is his appointment for?'

'Four-thirty.'

'Right, I'm on my way. I'll pick you both up at four.'

'There's no need, Damon. I can manage on my own.' Even as she said the words she ached for him. But she had stopped hoping for any kind of miracle in their relationship. If it wasn't for his concern over Mario, he wouldn't even have bothered talking to her now, never mind rush home.

'I know you can. But I'm still coming.'

He'd hung up before she could argue further.

However when Abbie went through and joined Elise in the kitchen she didn't have time to think again about Damon, because it was very obvious that Mario's condition was suddenly deteriorating fast. He was very lethargic, as if he was passing in and out of consciousness between bouts of crying.

'You know what? I don't think I can wait for that doctor's appointment, Elise,' Abbie said in panic as she took the child back into her arms. 'There's something really wrong with him.'

'Maybe you should take him to the hospital,' Elise agreed instantly. 'Shall I get Frederic to bring the car around?'

'Yes…and tell him to be quick.' Mario looked so weak, so unlike his usual robust self, that her heart squeezed with fear just watching him struggle to keep his eyes open. This wasn't good.

Damon arrived at the hospital ten minutes after the doctors had swept Mario away from her. She saw him striding down the corridor, his face gaunt with anxiety, and her heart welled up with emotion. Nothing from the past mattered at that moment, all that counted was the fact that she was so fiercely glad that he was here, as if somehow his very presence was going make their son better.

He looked up and saw her, and for just a moment there was a powerful expression of pain in his eyes. 'How is he?'

'The doctors have taken him away to do tests.' Abbie's voice caught with fear. 'Damon, he looks so ill I'm so afraid…'

She didn't get to finish her sentence, because the next

moment Damon had pulled her in close to his chest to hold her.

She melted against him, so glad to be in his arms again, and trying to draw strength from his presence. 'Do you think he'll be all right?' she whispered, desperate for reassurance. 'It all happened so quickly. I didn't know what to do.'

'You've done the best thing, getting him here so quickly, and he's going to be fine—he *has* to be fine.'

They stood for a while, just holding each other and holding on to that thought.

One of the doctors came through to the waiting room and looked around for her, and they broke apart. 'Is there any news?' Abbie asked anxiously.

The doctor didn't answer her immediately, but looked over at Damon. 'This is my husband, Damon Cyrenci.' Abbie introduced him quickly. 'How is our son? Is he going to be OK?'

'We are doing—more tests.' The doctor's English was halting, and Damon spoke to him in Italian.

It was deeply frustrating not to know what was being said. They were speaking so quickly that there was no way Abbie could even pick up on a few words, so she kept watching Damon's face nervously to try and figure out if this was good or bad.

It was hard to work out. Damon looked tense, but seemed like he was very much in control of the situation.

'So what is he telling you, Damon?' she asked as the doctor broke off to consult a chart in his hand.

'They are running a few more tests. Nothing is conclusive yet.'

'What are they testing him for?'

'Come on, let's sit down.' Damon nodded at the doctor and thanked him.

'But I want to see him, Damon. I need to be with him.'

'Not just yet. Come on, let's sit down.'

'Oh God, this is bad, isn't it?' She was suddenly terrified, and sank down into the chair that Damon had brought her towards.

'They suspect that he might have meningitis.' Damon sat down next to her and reached for her hand.

As he looked into her eyes, he saw the way her pupils dilated in fear at the word. 'Mario is really strong, he'll fight this.' Damon squeezed her hand. 'And the good thing is that you've got him here quickly.'

Although he was being positive, Abbie could see a muscle ticking along the side of his jaw. She looked down at the hand that held hers.

'I don't know what I'm going to do if I lose him, Damon, I can't bear it.' Her eyes misted with tears.

'We are not going to lose him.' Damon squeezed her hand tightly. 'He is receiving expert care, and the results of the tests aren't even back yet, so let's not cross bridges until we have to, hmm?'

She bit down on her lips and nodded. She knew he was right, but it was so hard not to let her imagination start running ahead.

They seemed to sit there for ages like that, just holding hands.

A nurse came by and asked if they would like a coffee, but they both refused.

'It's going to be all right, Abbie,' Damon said softly. He stroked a thumb over the back of her hand. 'He's a survivor, like his mother.'

She tried to smile, but couldn't. The touch of his hand against hers was so wonderful, so deeply comforting and reassuring, and yet so painful. Because if it hadn't been for their mutual love of Mario he wouldn't be holding her like this.

Damon looked down at the fragile hand in his and felt more helpless than he had ever felt in his life. He wanted to take away her pain, make this better, and have his son back in his arms.

The last few hours had been hell. Finding John Newland in his house like that had been a shock. Hearing their conversation had been even more shocking.

At first he hadn't been able to take it in. Part of him wondered angrily if it had all been staged, if somehow Abbie had known that he would come back to the house. But how could she have known?

And she had looked so scared. His heart had wrenched when he'd seen that look on her face, that anguish in her eyes. He'd had to get out of the house, had to take stock and think about things deeply. He didn't want to make any more mistakes, because he'd already made enough to last a lifetime.

A few doctors walked towards the door, and Damon and Abbie both looked up anxiously, but the doctors didn't come in. They were talking to the receptionist outside.

'This is hell,' Abbie grated, and he squeezed her hand even tighter.

The doctor who had spoken to them earlier suddenly appeared in the doorway and they both got to their feet.

This time the doctor smiled at Abbie. 'It is—how do you say?—good news.'

'Thank God.' Relief flooded through Abbie, and she leaned weakly against Damon as she listened to him questioning the doctor more closely in his native language.

'He has a viral infection, Abbie, but it is not meningitis and it can be treated,' he translated for her swiftly. 'They say he'll be fine in a few days.'

'Thank you.' Abbie smiled at the doctor, her eyes shimmering with gratitude.

Then impulsively she turned and went into Damon's arms.

It was so wonderful to be close to him, and the feelings of happiness and relief mingled with the sharp pain of knowing that this bond they shared was only one of mutual love for their son—nothing else.

'Can we see him?' Hastily she pulled away from him. Now that the worst was over and Mario was on the road to recovery, she knew that she couldn't allow herself the luxury of being in his arms.

CHAPTER TWELVE

ABBIE stepped outside the hospital front door and took a deep breath of the early-morning air. She and Damon had sat next to Mario's bed throughout the night, neither of them wanting to leave until their son's fever had broken.

Finally, at six o'clock that morning, Mario had smiled at her and she had seen the healthy colour returning to his skin. Then he had settled down into a peaceful and exhausted sleep. That was when she had allowed Damon to persuade her to go home.

She felt worn out as she waited for Frederic to bring the car around. The emotional turmoil of the last few days, added to her fears for Mario, had taken its toll. She knew she probably looked washed out, and she felt wretched. But she didn't intend to be away from Mario for long. She would just have a shower and freshen up and then go straight back. For one thing, Damon deserved a break as well. Sitting across the hospital bed from him, she had realised that the worry over Mario plus losing a night's sleep had also affected him—he'd also looked shattered and drawn.

The car arrived, and as Abbie settled into the comfortable seats she closed her eyes. It had been such a strange night. She and Damon had been at pains to be polite with each other after the worst had passed. It had been as if they had never held each other moments earlier or sat holding hands.

He probably was still furious with her for allowing her father into his house. They couldn't go on like this, she realised sadly. It was tearing her apart and it was probably tearing him apart, too. He didn't trust her—*couldn't* trust her. The situation was no good for either of them.

But what was the alternative—a divorce? For the first time she allowed herself to admit that might be where they were headed. She raked a hand in anguish through her hair as she imagined that situation—a polite distance from each other maintained at all times, except in periods of emergency.

At least she knew he would be there for his son no matter what. But living in close proximity to him like that and yet not being with him would be torture.

But what choice did she have? If they divorced she couldn't go back to St Lucia. She'd lost everything there, and anyway it wouldn't be fair to deny Mario regular access to his father. And it was obvious how deeply Damon felt about his son. Even after the doctor had told them everything was going to be all right, the bleak expression hadn't completely left his eyes.

No, her only option if they decided on a divorce would be to try and get a flat and a job somewhere nearby. She didn't want it to end like this, she really didn't. The pain in her heart felt overwhelming. But to love someone and know that there was no hope of them ever loving you back was also too painful to bear.

The car pulled up outside the house, and she went inside. Everything was quiet and the kitchen was deserted.

'Elise?' she called to the housekeeper as she went through to the hallway, but there was no reply. Maybe she'd gone for a lie down, Abbie reflected. She knew she had been very worried about Mario, and although Damon had rung her as soon as they had known he was going to be OK she had probably had little sleep.

Going upstairs, Abbie stripped off in the bedroom and went for a shower. It was bliss to stand under the hot, pounding water.

She was just pulling on her dressing gown when she heard a noise from downstairs.

'Elise?' She opened the bedroom door and looked out. 'Elise, is that you?'

'No, it's me.' To her surprise Damon appeared at the top of the stairs. 'Elise arrived at the hospital a few moments after you left, so I decided to take the opportunity for a quick break.'

'I see.' He did look like he needed a break—in fact, he looked terrible. 'But everything is all right with Mario, isn't it?' she asked anxiously.

'Yes. I saw the doctor again before I left, and he told me they might discharge him later today.'

'Thank God for that.' Abbie smiled at him tremulously.

'Yes.'

For a moment there was an odd silence between them. His eyes moved down over her figure. 'You were wearing that dressing gown when I arrived at your door in St Lucia,' he recalled suddenly. 'Seems like a lifetime ago.'

She nodded. 'Well, a lot has happened since then. Marriage, and now…' She trailed off brokenly. 'Now it's all such a mess.'

'You want a divorce, don't you?' He asked the question bluntly, and there was a very sombre look in his eyes now.

She yearned to tell him that a divorce was the last thing she wanted—that what she wanted was for them to make things work, and for him to trust her. But pride kept her silent. What was the point in telling him that? He wouldn't believe her anyway. When he'd found her father in his home, he had probably come to the conclusion that he couldn't continue with this charade.

So she shrugged helplessly. 'I think we both know deep down that we can't continue like this—' she whispered brokenly.

'Abbie, I can't bear it,' he cut across her suddenly. 'I know I have absolutely no right to ask you this—but I really can't bear for you to leave.'

Abbie frowned. She'd never heard that raw note in his voice before. He'd always been so much in control of the situation, and of her. 'Well, you know I can't go anywhere unless you allow me to leave. I have nowhere to go, Damon...' Her voice broke for a moment.

Damon raked a hand through his hair. He couldn't believe that he had done this to her—trapped her here against her will—used her.

Yesterday when he'd left the house he'd needed to put space and time between them, had needed to be alone when the blinkers had finally lifted from his eyes—because the guilt had been so damn overwhelming that he just couldn't bear it.

Overhearing the conversation between Abbie and her father yesterday had made him sick to his stomach. Hearing the truth had opened a pit of guilt and despair inside him that he didn't think he would ever be able to close. Now he knew the reason for the sadness in her eyes when she looked at him: she was innocent of all the charges he had laid before her. She was as much a victim of what had happened in Vegas as his father had been.

The conversation had confirmed what he'd wanted to believe. She didn't have a bad, selfish or mercenary bone in her body.

But the revelation had come too late.

He'd hurt her so much, trapped her in a marriage she didn't want, in a place she didn't want to be.

She had tried valiantly to make the best of the situation, and to make things work, but she didn't want to be here.

He remembered the way he'd tried to punish her—the way he'd talked to her, the way he had taken her body so ruthlessly. And he hated himself.

'Damon?' The soft, questioning note in her voice tore into him. 'Damon, I need you to believe me when I tell you I didn't invite my father to this house—'

'I know you didn't invite him. I heard every word.' His voice cracked for a moment under the weight of emotion that was tearing him up inside.

'You heard?' Her voice was stiff with disbelief. 'But you blamed me—you walked away.'

'I couldn't bear to look at you.' His voice was husky with a strange note that she couldn't place. 'I hated myself too much for what I'd done to you. And when I looked at you and saw the distress in your eyes… Oh, Abbie, I couldn't bear it— couldn't bear the knowledge of what I'd put you through—of what you'd been through before I met you.'

For a moment she stood silently, hardly daring to believe what she was hearing. 'So you believe I didn't lie to you? You believe I would never have done anything deliberately to hurt you? That my father forced me into a situation that I didn't want?'

As he listened to the pain in her voice, Damon's heart smote him once more with the horrific guilt of what he had put her through, what he had accused her of. 'Yes, I believe it,' he whispered. 'And I'm so sorry, Abbie. I've behaved so badly towards you. I believed the worst—I wanted revenge… And all the time you were an innocent victim of your father as well.' He shook his head, and she could hear the self-disgust in his voice. 'Abbie, why didn't you tell me about your mother?'

'I tried…' Tears sparkled in her eyes. The relief that he knew the truth was so tremendous, as if a weight of a hundred boulders had lifted from her. 'But you didn't want to listen or believe anything I said about the past. And it hurt so much, Damon, to try and talk about something so deeply personal and painful and have everything I said twisted and scornfully dismissed…'

'I should have listened and believed you, but I was so sure that you were lying—'

'Damon, it's OK.' She cut across him, hating to hear his voice crack like that. 'I understand why you couldn't believe me.' She took a step closer. 'All the evidence was against me. And I know you had trust issues, as well, from your past.'

Even now, after the way he had hurt her, she could still find it in her heart to excuse him. Somehow the fact that she was so gently forgiving made him feel worse. He'd got it wrong so badly—had ignored all the voices of caution and believed the worst of her. He didn't know if he would ever forgive himself, let alone expect her forgiveness. Hearing her tell her father how this situation had ruined her life had been gutwrenching.

'I don't deserve your forgiveness, Abbie. But I'm going to put everything right, I promise. I'll tear up the prenuptial agreement for a start. You can have whatever you want.'

'You don't have to do that. I don't want anything.'

'I know you don't want anything! But I need to do that—don't you understand? I couldn't live with myself knowing…' He trailed off. 'And I'll move out of the house, if that is what you really want, while we decide how best to proceed.'

'Move out?' Her voice was cold suddenly, and the feeling of relief inside her quickly started to turn to fear. 'Why would you do that?'

'Because I want to do the right thing by you and make amends.' He broke off and spoke in Italian for a moment.

'Damon, I don't understand.' She shook her head.

'I'm saying I always thought of myself as an honourable man, and I've treated you so badly that I'm ashamed. I've forced you into a marriage that you don't want.'

'Damon, I…'

'There's no excuse for what I've done. Yes, I wanted to give Mario the best and most secure of family lives, but instead I've just brought misery and acted selfishly.'

Abbie stared up at him, her heart thundering painfully. 'So you want a divorce?'

'No! That's the last thing I want, Abbie!' His voice grated harshly and there was such torment in his eyes as he looked at her that she wanted to reach out to him. 'I'm a proud man, Abbie—possibly too proud.' His lips twisted cynically. 'But I'm not too proud to beg you now. Please don't end our marriage.'

'Damon, don't!' She took a step closer to him. She hated to see him like this. 'You didn't need to beg. I know how much you love Mario. I won't take him away from you. I couldn't live with myself, knowing how much he means to you—'

'Yes, he means a lot to me.' Damon reached out and touched her face. 'But so do you, Abbie.'

'Do I?' The heart-wrenching question made Damon's insides turn over with regret. He murmured something in Sicilian, before shaking his head. 'I've been such a fool where you are concerned. I believed what John Newland told me about you, when he was an obvious charlatan.'

'Well, he could be very convincing,' Abbie murmured. 'When my mother got sick and I had to ring him for help, I believed for one crazy moment that he felt some compassion for her circumstances.' She shook her head. 'But that man doesn't appear to have an ounce of compassion in his soul.'

'Unlike his daughter—who has too much, who has forgiven me against all the odds.'

'You were hurt by him too.'

'Abbie, can we try again?'

The sudden question made her heart almost stop beating.

'I've been such an idiot,' he rasped. 'I've never deserved you. And I know I've made a mess of things. But we are married now…and we are good together, aren't we?'

The question tore her up.

'You mean the chemistry is still good between us,' she corrected him huskily.

'Yes.' For a second his eyes moved towards her lips. 'There is no denying that. Is there?'

She shook her head; there was no way she could deny that.

'And we've got the most wonderful son in the world who we both adore.'

She smiled at that. 'Yes.'

'So let me try and make amends by being the best husband you could wish for.'

For a second Abbie's eyes shimmered with tears. She wanted to say yes, she wanted to go back into his arms so badly. But she knew she couldn't. She just couldn't give herself to him again, knowing that the love between them wasn't there. That he would only be doing this for his son. It was too painful, and she loved him too much to be able to bear it.

'Damon, we were good together, and the chemistry between us is strong.' Her voice shook alarmingly. 'But it's not enough.'

'Don't say that, Abbie, please!' His eyes held hers steadily. 'I'm nothing without you. Please say you will be my wife for ever this time. For richer or poorer, in sickness and in health, all the days of our lives I want to cherish you and love you and be with you.'

'You want to love me?' Her heart skipped a few beats.

He nodded. 'Abbie, I love you more than you could ever know. I've just been too proud, and…' His lips twisted in a rueful way. 'Maybe too frightened by my feelings for you to admit it—even to myself.'

Abbie couldn't find her voice to say anything for a moment; she was too overwhelmed by what he had just told her. 'You really love me?' she managed at last. 'Really?'

'With all my heart.'

A tear trickled down her pale face. 'Damon, I don't know what to say, I…'

'Just say that we can stay together and give our marriage a chance. That's all I'm asking for, Abbie. I know you don't love me—in fact I know you've downright disliked me sometimes, and I've deserved it. I've said some terrible things, done some terrible things, and I'm deeply sorry. But let me try and make things up to you, please.'

'I've never disliked you,' she murmured. 'It's just something I said to cover my real feelings. To lie to myself.'

He frowned. 'But I've made you so very sad sometimes.' He wiped her tears away with a tender hand. 'On our wedding day, for instance, I made you cry.' His voice cracked with fierce emotion. 'I hated myself for that.'

'I didn't cry because you made me sad, Damon,' she whispered softly. 'I cried because I realised how much I loved you. I've always loved you. Right from that first moment we met in Las Vegas and I looked into your eyes out by the swimming pool.'

'You loved me?' His voice sounded strange as if he hardly dared to believe what she had said. 'But I heard you tell your father that what he had done had ruined your life. That everything hadn't turned out for the best.'

'I was talking about the fact that he'd turned you against me—that we had wasted precious years apart, that even now you didn't trust me. And I loved you so much.'

'Oh my darling.' He pulled her close and held her. 'My darling Abigail. I'm so sorry…for putting you through that torment. I misunderstood, and all I could think was that I had ruined your life by bringing you here. I felt so wretchedly guilty that I had to get out of the house—I didn't know what to do, where to put myself.'

She leaned against him and wound her arms around his neck. 'Damon, I love you, and I want to make this marriage work more than anything in this world.'

'I want that too, more than you will ever know.' He pulled away from her for a moment and then kissed her, a long, sensual, burning kiss that made her heart turn over with longing. He murmured something to her in Italian.

'I don't understand what you are saying,' she whispered.

'I'm saying that I love you so much,' he whispered hungrily. 'Need you so much.'

'Me too.'

He kissed her again and then, sweeping her up into his arms, carried her back into the bedroom.

Abbie laughed tremulously. 'We haven't got time for this, Damon, we need to get back to the hospital.'

'Yes, but first we have some more making-up to do.'

'And secondly?' She looked up at him playfully as he put her down on the bed.

'Secondly there are a few Sicilian phrases I need to run by you. Phrases like "I love you" and "I adore you" and "I will always be here for you"…'

'I'd love to learn those words, Damon.' She reached up to kiss him, knowing that for the first time in her life she was truly home, truly happy.

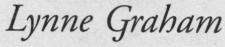
HP12787

HARLEQUIN Presents

MISTRESS TO A MILLIONAIRE

She's his in the bedroom, but he can't buy her love...

**Showered with diamonds,
draped in exquisite lingerie,
whisked around the world...
The ultimate fantasy becomes a reality
in**

Sharon Kendrick's

BOUGHT FOR THE SICILIAN BILLIONAIRE'S BED

Available Janary 2009
Book #2789

**Live the dream with more
Mistress to a Millionaire titles
by your favorite authors**

Coming soon!

REQUEST YOUR FREE BOOKS!

2 FREE NOVELS PLUS 2 FREE GIFTS!

PASSION GUARANTEED SEDUCTION

YES! Please send me 2 FREE Harlequin Presents® novels and my 2 FREE gifts (gifts are worth about $10). After receiving them, if I don't wish to receive any more books, I can return the shipping statement marked "cancel". If I don't cancel, I will receive 6 brand-new novels every month and be billed just $4.05 per book in the U.S. or $4.74 per book in Canada, plus 25¢ shipping and handling per book and applicable taxes, if any*. That's a savings of close to 15% off the cover price! I understand that accepting the 2 free books and gifts places me under no obligation to buy anything. I can always return a shipment and cancel at any time. Even if I never buy another book, the two free books and gifts are mine to keep forever.

106 HDN ERRW 306 HDN ERRL

Name	(PLEASE PRINT)	
Address		Apt. #
City	State/Prov.	Zip/Postal Code

Signature (if under 18, a parent or guardian must sign)

Mail to the **Harlequin Reader Service:**
IN U.S.A.: P.O. Box 1867, Buffalo, NY 14240-1867
IN CANADA: P.O. Box 609, Fort Erie, Ontario L2A 5X3

Not valid to current subscribers of Harlequin Presents books.

Want to try two free books from another line?
Call 1-800-873-8635 or visit www.morefreebooks.com.

* Terms and prices subject to change without notice. N.Y. residents add applicable sales tax. Canadian residents will be charged applicable provincial taxes and GST. Offer not valid in Quebec. This offer is limited to one order per household. All orders subject to approval. Credit or debit balances in a customer's account(s) may be offset by any other outstanding balance owed by or to the customer. Please allow 4 to 6 weeks for delivery. Offer available while quantities last.

Your Privacy: Harlequin Books is committed to protecting your privacy. Our Privacy Policy is available online at www.eHarlequin.com or upon request from the Reader Service. From time to time we make our lists of customers available to reputable third parties who may have a product or service of interest to you. If you would prefer we not share your name and address, please check here. ☐

HP08R

HARLEQUIN *Presents*

EXCLUSIVELY HIS

Back in his bed—and he's better than ever!

Whether you shared his bed for one night or five
years, certain men are impossible to forget!
He might be your ex, but when you're back in his
bed, the passion is not just hot, it's scorching!

CLAIMED BY THE
ROGUE BILLIONAIRE
by **Trish Wylie**

Available January 2009
Book #2794

*Look for more Exclusively His novels
from Harlequin Presents in 2009!*

You're invited to join our Tell Harlequin Reader Panel!

By joining our new reader panel you will:

- Receive Harlequin® books—they are FREE and yours to keep with no obligation to purchase anything!
- Participate in fun online surveys
- Exchange opinions and ideas with women just like you
- Have a say in our new book ideas and help us publish the best in women's fiction

In addition, you will have a chance to win great prizes and receive special gifts! See Web site for details. Some conditions apply. Space is limited.

To join, visit us at
www.TellHarlequin.com.